OUT
OF
LOVE

OUT
OF
LOVE

a novel
by

Roy MacSkimming

Cormorant Books

Published with the assistance of the Canada Council,
the Ontario Arts Council, and the Government of Ontario
through the Ministry of Culture and Communications.

Front cover from printed paper, acrylic, etc. on paper,
Flying Fish, by Courtney Andersen, 1985, 43.5 x 38.5 cm.,
from the collection of The Canada Council Art Bank,
courtesy of the artist.

Cover design by Artcetera Graphics, Dunvegan, Ontario.

Typeset by Moveable Type Inc., Toronto, Ontario.

Published by Cormorant Books Inc.,
RR #1, Dunvegan, Ontario, Canada K0C 1J0.

Printed and bound in Canada.

Canadian Cataloguing in Publication Data

MacSkimming, Roy, 1944–
    Out of love

ISBN 0-920953-88-3

    I. Title.

PS8575.S53088 1993   C813'.54   C93-090038-3
PR9199.3.M33088 1993

For
Graham
and
Andrew

At first…we seek to supplement the emptiness of our individuality through love, and for a brief moment enjoy the illusion of completeness. But it is only an illusion. For this strange creature, which we thought would join us to the body of the world, succeeds at last in separating us most thoroughly from it.

– Lawrence Durrell

1

I dislike getting telegrams, or messages of any sort, from the government. This one arrived at my apartment a little after nine in the evening—in my apprehension I forgot to tip the messenger:

NICHOLAS ALAN URQUHART COMMITTED TO CIVIL DETENTION ATHENS GREECE 3 AUGUST 1974 STOP CIRCUMSTANCES UNCLEAR STOP AWAITING TRIAL CHARGES UNSPECIFIED STOP DETAILS TO FOLLOW WHEN AVAILABLE

It was signed GILLES PAQUETTE DEPARTMENT OF EXTERNAL AFFAIRS. There was a number I could call between eight-thirty a.m. and four-thirty p.m., Monday through Friday.

Details to follow. When available.

After the first panic had ebbed, I sat down slowly in the living room. I took air deep into my lungs, exhaled, and tried to imagine what in God's name Nick could have done to get himself thrown in jail in Athens.

Theft? Hardly.

Reckless driving? Unlikely: he drove well for a twenty-year-old. I'd taught him, using the parks and parking lots of Toronto for practice, testing fatherly patience against his native resistance to learning anything from me.

Drugs. I wondered if he smoked, or dropped acid, or whatever. After two years of living apart, there would be many things I didn't know about him.

I grabbed an office memo pad from my desk and started making a list. It was a way of getting some kind of handle on the situation, and it calmed me a little.

Assault.

Shoplifting.

Bad cheques.

Breaking and entering.

Fraud.

I crossed all of these out. None of them made any sense whatsoever applied to Nick.

Insulting a police officer. Possible. I put a question mark beside that one.

Public mischief?

Trespassing?

Walking out of a restaurant without leaving enough money, then getting into an argument over the bill, something like that: a misunderstanding about the currency, the exchange rate, the language. Greek was awfully difficult. Maybe he'd broken the law inadvertently, out of ignorance. Or been maliciously accused and couldn't explain himself. Or was I just making excuses for him?

I abandoned my list and returned to the telegram, lying where I'd dropped it on the coffee table like the body of some small, dead, but still-menacing animal. The message was cryptic, opaque, bereft of details or context.

August 3rd had been two days ago. Nick had actually been locked up for *two whole days*. Jesus. How was he handling it? What he was feeling? Worst of all, why hadn't they informed me sooner?

The telegram's use of his middle name made it all uncomfortably precise, irrefutably official. Alan after my old man, dead these many years, upright hard-working Scot, pillar of the benighted little community where I'd grown up. Nicholas after Ayios Nikolaos, the Aegean port where Una and I had stayed when we were free and broke. Where we'd conceived him in a fisherman's stone house on the north coast of Crete. In a sense, Nick had been trying to get home.

The strange thing was that Greece hadn't even been on his itinerary. He was supposed to be in Italy now, backpacking among sun-dried hill towns — Siena, Arezzo, Perugia, Assisi. But then, he hadn't updated me on his travel plans recently. In fact, he hadn't written for exactly two months and five days.

8

This silence was a big change from the beginning of his *Wanderjahr*, the previous autumn. Then he'd written practically every week, long rambling letters full of news and impressions, practically stream-of-consciousness, from England, Wales, Scotland, followed by postcards from the Continent. The postcards hadn't been as good as his letters—I'd missed the spontaneous flow of his moods and thoughts, his unguarded and possibly unconscious revelations—but at least the cards contained words in his own hand and, nearly as good, images of the places he'd been visiting.

I loved picturing Nick—tall, fair-haired, nearsighted, slightly stooped—inhabiting European landscapes. Hiking up a fragrant Provençal hillside. Entering a dim Spanish cathedral. Eating frugally at a sidewalk café. Exploring some Roman neighbourhood. All things I'd done myself once, reassuring images. But locked up in a Greek jail: I couldn't picture *that*. I could hardly begin to think about it.

When even the postcards had stopped coming, sometime after his twentieth birthday, celebrated (with what companions?) somewhere in France, I tried not to worry too much. He's busy, I told myself. Lots to see and do. I continued sending my own letters to the sequence of American Express offices where he'd said he'd be checking for mail—Barcelona, Toulouse, Marseilles, Milan, Florence, Rome—and continued feeling reassured every time I saw that the cheque I'd enclosed with my letter had been cashed by American Express, endorsed on the back with Nick's inimitably eccentric signature. The last cheque, returned two weeks earlier, had been dated July 1 and cashed in Rome.

Finally, unable to deny my anxieties any longer, I'd phoned Una—just once. I had to know if she'd heard anything. If, in other words, Nick had found it possible to write to his mother but not me.

No, Una was in the same state of ignorance I was. Nonetheless, she thought it was still too early to panic. He was an adult now, she reminded me in her cool, level, professional voice, we couldn't treat him like a child any more. She'd always considered me overprotective.

Now the telegram showed I'd been right to worry. Cold

comfort. Yet I'd never expected anything like this—at home, Nick's only brushes with the law had involved relatively benign Toronto cops on horseback during anti-war demonstrations, and a couple of unpaid parking summonses I'd paid after he left on his student charter-flight to London. Nick was a lot of things, intellectually arrogant, emotionally self-absorbed, fitfully generous, even furtively affectionate from time to time, but he was no criminal.

To make things worse, Greece was going through one of its periodic political crises. I knew from experience how chaotic the country became at such times. The military junta had just collapsed, there was a risk of war with Turkey. Ironically, hundreds of people were in the process of being released from prison, right when Nick was being locked up. It was perverse. A sudden access of freedom, I reflected gloomily, is always a volatile and dangerous time.

2

I dialled the number in the telegram on the stroke of eight-thirty next morning. Listening to the dial tone, I realized it was already three-thirty p.m. for Nick. As if he were slipping farther away with every hour.

A secretary said Mr. Paquette had left on his holidays yesterday, but would be back in two weeks. Would I care to leave a message?

I gave her the name of a deputy director at External Affairs I'd met at a book launching once. Paquette's secretary connected me with *his* secretary, who explained her boss was on secondment to another department at the moment, but would I like to speak to the acting deputy director? I said I would. In that case, she said, she'd take my number and have him call me tomorrow when he returned from Montreal.

I asked for Paquette's secretary again and, as patiently as I could, explained my need for immediate news about my son's situation in Greece. She'd like to help, she said, but unfortunately knew nothing about the case. She would, however, connect me with an officer, Mr. Rutledge, who had authority to discuss "the file" in Mr. Paquette's absence.

Mr. Rutledge sounded young. I went over my story. He asked me to hold the line while he went off in search of the file—as if this were some dusty archival matter from the distant past, instead of a clear and present emergency—and returned several minutes later, having apparently scanned the file's contents in the meantime.

"Does it say what Nick is charged with?"

"Actually, Mr. Urquhart, no. For some reason we don't seem to have that information."

"Good Lord."

"Well, yes. It's rather unusual."

"Is there a court date?"

"Apparently not. Or if there is, it hasn't been communicated to us."

"Then what about bail? Can I wire funds to get him released until a hearing?"

"*That* might be possible. You never can tell. We'll certainly check into it for you," he said brightly.

"Please do that. At once, if you don't mind. I don't want Nick spending any more time in jail than necessary." I could just visualize the situation over there: the dirt, the neglect, the confusion, the institutionalized obstacles, the appalling red tape. "Of course he'll need someone to represent him. Does the embassy arrange for legal services? Or should I?"

"Our post in Athens will cover that. Now, at this point in time, Mr. Urquhart, they may have to—"

"I want to send a telegram, let him know—"

"Please understand, sir, we'll do *everything* we can. But with the troubles over there right now, it's extremely difficult communicating with the Greek authorities. As soon as we have any information—"

"Have the Greeks stopped answering the telephone?" I was finding Mr. Rutledge's caution very hard to take. And it was obvious no one at External had followed up on Nick's case. "I mean, we *pay* you people to look after Canadians abroad."

In the silence that followed, I considered flying up to Ottawa to deal with Mr. Rutledge in person, going over his head if necessary to get some action. I realized it would just be a waste of time. The best way of helping Nick was to go to Athens myself.

Mr. Rutledge allowed as how that might "move things along", assuming I could get a flight. The Greek airports had reopened after the war scare with Turkey, but it was impossible to say how long they'd stay open. "At the same time, my duty is to advise you such a course of action could be quite dangerous at the moment. Greece and Turkey are refusing to negotiate over Cyprus. There's still a possibility of fighting on the mainland."

Ye gods, I thought. If he thinks it's dangerous for me,

what does he imagine it's like for Nick? I asked Mr. Rutledge to suggest someone I could see at the embassy in Athens, and he gave me his one piece of information that would turn out to be crucial: the name of the consular officer who'd sent the original telex about Nick to Ottawa — an Eleni Diamantides.

I phoned Canadian Pacific to book the first available flight to Athens. The ticket agent said the government's advisory against travel to Greece had resulted in some cancellations. I could leave the next day at six p.m.

That left one more call to make before leaving for the office. I dialled Una's number — once my own, and practically the only thing about our former matrimonial home she hadn't changed — to let her know what was happening. No answer. I tried her office number and, to my relief, got her in person on the first ring, announcing herself, "Una Urquhart", in the absence of her secretary. It startled me to realize she was still using her married name. Una wasn't a fan of mine, for reasons I'd long regretted but couldn't do much about.

She listened as I explained. I could feel her tension mounting over the phone.

"Oh God," she said finally. "But well, I suppose you're right, going over there is the only thing to do. Those External types take forever. They have to get five approvals just to send a telex." Una worked in government herself.

"Do you want to come with me?"

"Me? What for?"

"Two heads might be better than one."

She was silent a moment. "I don't know, Jim ... even assuming I could get away from here.... Wouldn't you rather handle it on your own?"

"Not necessarily."

"Besides, it could take weeks. You'll probably have to come back before Nick's even released. *Then* I could go over — we might have to take turns or something."

"I hope not."

She wanted me to phone or wire her from Athens as soon as I had any news. She gave me the telex number at her office.

13

"Well, listen, I know how upsetting this is for you," she said, bending a little. "It's terrible imagining him in jail and everything. But it's probably just a mistake. He'll probably be okay in the end, don't you think? I mean, Nick's a lot tougher than you or I realize."

"Sure."

"And listen—Jim? You be careful too, okay? Greece doesn't sound very safe right now."

More perversity. Her concern for me was so atypical, so unexpected, it threw me for a loss. It reminded me how incomplete I felt without her, a floater—no ground beneath my feet.

Not only that, but Nick himself had been infinitely safer when he'd been in Athens six years earlier, in 1968, with Una and me: the three of us a family on holiday during the dictatorship.

3

During the overnight flight to Athens, I had plenty of time to think. I wished I'd taken more time, been cooler-headed, more patient. Maybe I could have devised some constructive way to work for Nick's release through the government. Maybe Michaelis could have helped.

Michaelis might have advised me on the route to take through the byzantine legal system; could have recommended a lawyer over there to handle the case. But when I'd phoned him earlier that day, both his lines at home had been busy, and when I'd called his number at the university, the departmental secretary said he'd already cleaned out his desk and wouldn't be back. Michaelis and his aides and family were busy, she explained, preparing for their return to Greece. After that, I'd been too rushed to try him again before leaving for the airport.

I'd first encountered Michaelis Kastri in autumn 1968, during the long-planned family holiday in Greece. After doing battle with our consciences, Una and I had decided to return despite the dictatorship.

Every Greek town and village was defaced by propaganda then: posters and billboards portraying the nation as a demure maiden in a virginal white dress, protected by helmeted soldiers. Huge electrified signs proclaimed "Long Live the 21st of April!", the date of the military takeover. But in the end, we rationalized that we had as much right to be there as the Colonels. Everything had begun for us in Greece. It was the land where we'd adventured, met by hazard, made love within the hour, lived together in the stone house overlooking the Sea of Crete. Made Nick.

We'd been talking about returning for fifteen years, well before the army had seized power, but somehow had never found the time or money. Yet if we didn't do it then, when would we? Who knew how long the junta might last? And before long, Nick would be too old to want to travel with us. So we reasoned. At least I did. I didn't pay enough attention to the fact that neither Una nor Nick was showing as much enthusiasm for the trip as I.

To my mind, the timing was undeniably right. It was early enough in the school year that Nick would miss little of importance; he'd always excelled academically, and would be able to catch up without any trouble. Una's MBA program would begin in January, and I had a feeling she'd be uninterested in anything else once she started working on her degree. As for me, I'd seen all my fall books through the press; that opened a window of three weeks or so before I had to tackle the spring titles. I ran the editorial side of a publishing house specializing in political books and history and biography, plus the odd politically correct novel to keep things interesting, and I was long overdue for a holiday.

It seems perfectly obvious now, but at the time I failed — refused, rather — to recognize that trip for what it was: a last attempt to recapture the past before the deluge.

*   *   *

We stayed in our old haunt, the Kimon, a small and some-what comfortless hotel on Apollonos Street. Nick thought it an odd choice, but it had an excellent location — right on the edge of the Plaka, around the corner from the Orthodox cathedral — in addition to its sentimental appeal.

One evening near the end of the trip, the three of us ate dinner at an open-air restaurant in a leafy square in the Plaka, then retired to the hotel to read. Vaguely at first, we began to hear the low murmur of people gathering down in the streets. As the sound grew louder, Una and I collected Nick from his room next to ours and went outside for a look.

We stood at the edge of a crowd that was swelling every minute, filling the street in front of the cathedral: hundreds of people gathering in the warm darkness, watching impatiently, waiting. Finally a gleaming black automobile nosed its way out of the shadows. Falling silent, the crowd parted to let it pass. When the hearse came to a halt, dark-suited men climbed out and removed a coffin draped with the blue and white Greek flag and, without warning, like thunder on a clear night, a terrible applause erupted from the onlookers.

Una and I exchanged looks. She'd just washed her auburn hair, which she wore short at the time, and I could smell the pine scent lingering on her scalp. She leaned behind Nick and moistly whispered "Kastri!" into my ear.

We'd heard the rumour that George Kastri had died of heart failure that morning. The junta had evidently decreed a news blackout on the funeral plans, even on the body's resting place, to prevent demonstrations, but in Athens it's impossible to keep anything secret for long. There must have been nearly a thousand people there, every one of whom continued applauding long after the coffin disappeared inside the cathedral. They didn't care if they offended the Colonels: all the better to express their grief. And nobody tried to silence them.

Kastri, who had been under house arrest for several months, had been the leading liberal statesman in Greece for decades—a patriot and a democrat, two qualities not always combined in a Greek leader. To his admirers he was a populist visionary, triumphing over imprisonment and exile to lead the nation towards democracy; to his detractors he was a demagogue, an unprincipled opportunist. But everyone knew that when the Colonels had seized power in 1967 and cancelled the elections, they'd been blocking the old man's final return to power.

Eventually the crowd drifted away, so we returned to the hotel; there would be no further incidents that night. But two days later, when Kastri's funeral took place, Una and Nick and I were back in the street outside the cathedral, by now feeling part of the drama. This time hundreds of uniformed policemen were on duty. Prepared for several thousand mourners, they found half a million jamming the sidestreets fanning out from the church. Clearly their orders were to crush any political outburst before it inflamed the mob. Whenever a lone voice broke into a chant—"*Kas-tri!*" "*Di-mok-ra-ti-a!*"—the cops on the fringes of the mob waded in, white truncheons swinging.

To me, wedged in tight between Una and Nick, my arms wrapped around their warm waists, the mob pushing us fore and aft, it didn't seem especially dangerous, no more than it had two nights earlier. We were protected by our neutral status as foreigners—harmless, blameless, a nice Canadian family.

A short, nondescript man in a dark suit plucked me out of my neutrality. Seizing my elbow, he demanded in heavily accented English: "You know what is this? You understand what is happening?"

I said I did.

"George Kastri still lives," he said urgently, "his son Michaelis still fights for us—still fights for the democracy in Greece! We hear him! Every week on BBC shortwave!"

His eyes locked onto mine, willing me to carry this information back to wherever I'd come from—such is the psychic imprisonment of people inside a dictatorship—then, looking suddenly alarmed, he backed away from me and melted into the crowd.

It was the first time I'd ever heard of Michaelis Kastri. Twelve months later, he and I had become colleagues in Toronto. We were even on our way, I imagined, to becoming friends.

*   *   *

My flight to Athens was one of the first since the official state of emergency had ended. My fellow passengers didn't seem the least bit unnerved by the continuing danger of war. Nearly all Greeks returning home for a visit, they became increasingly festive and exalted as we approached their homeland after the brief transatlantic night, despite having had only a couple of hours' sleep. They'd found some new source of energy to fuel the smoke-filled conversations held up and down the aisle high over the Ionian Sea.

Entire dynasties from Toronto's Greek community were on board. One extended family, from great-grandparents to babes in arms, occupied several rows on both sides of the aisle. Many of the men on board were of military age; some may have been self-exiled for political reasons, and now were seizing the opportunity to return. Under Greek law they could be drafted into the army, even if they'd become Canadian citizens in the meantime, but they'd be perfectly aware of that—aware, too, that there had already been a call-up of military reservists—and they wouldn't care. If asked, they'd have said they welcomed a chance to fight. The Greeks were all a little crazy when it came to the Turks.

I'd read every paper and newsmagazine I could find on the plane for reports out of Athens. It was clearer than ever that Nick couldn't have picked a worse time to be there.

The Colonels had surrendered power several days ago. They hadn't been toppled by a popular uprising, a democratic revolution in the cradle of democracy—nothing as heroic as that—they'd simply abdicated, quit, after a disastrous attempt to overthrow the government of Cyprus. They'd backed a coup against Archbishop Makarios, provoking Turkey to invade the island on the pretence of protecting the Turkish minority. Now the Turks occupied nearly half of Cyprus. Greece and Turkey were threatening to bomb each other's coastal ports and shipping, but so far nothing had come of the threats. Except that, overnight, Greece had been rid of its dictatorship.

Civilian politicians were trying to pick up the pieces in Athens. Former party leaders were arriving home from exile one by one. Soon, Michaelis would be among them. They had their work cut out for them: restoring civil authority, filling the constitutional vacuum, responding to the Turkish occupation, calming an exhilarated, angry, frightened population. A provisional government under former prime minister Karamanlis had been established to deal with it all. In the meantime, who was dealing with Nick?

19

*   *   *

After our return home from Greece in 1968, our family life had changed. It began taking a disquieting series of turnings — but disquieting, it seemed, only to me.

Nick became immediately absorbed once again in his personal life and private pastimes, his world of school and athletics and friends, as if we'd never been away. I felt excluded by him more than ever. This hurt more than I was willing to admit, since the holiday had brought us, ever so briefly, closer again. Rationally, I knew it was normal and healthy for him to want to go his own way at that point in his life; emotionally, it was a different matter.

Immediately, too, Una plunged straight into her MBA program, starting her research ahead of schedule. She couldn't wait to get at it — as if our return to Greece had been an unwelcome disruption of her real and overriding purpose in life. Although I was rather ashamed to admit it, this bothered me also. Unlike Una, I hadn't learned to accord a higher value to the present than the past.

So I tried to concentrate on the tasks at hand: writing catalogue copy, approving jacket designs, overseeing editorial work, attempting to keep skittish authors happy. But these activities didn't afford their usual rich satisfaction. In a random and barely conscious way, I was casting about for something, something I couldn't identify, which could bring the past forward into the present and fuse them into some sort of high purpose, to be a match for my wife's and my son's.

I asked one of my authors, a columnist at the *Star*, to check the paper's library for clippings about Michaelis Kastri. There wasn't much. Michaelis was still a relatively obscure figure in North America, in contrast to his growing celebrity in Europe. But the clippings did contain some rudimentary facts about him: he'd studied economics in London and Berkeley; he'd become a professor at Columbia and Chicago, noted for his studies of government economic planning; he'd sacrificed a successful academic career to return to Greece and enter politics, serving as a minister in his father's last

20

government in the mid-sixties; the Right had accused him of plotting with some young military officers to overthrow the monarchy; he'd been jailed for six months by the Colonels after they seized power. His release had come only after an intensive public campaign by his American wife, Catherine, and his former colleagues in the States, and now Michaelis and his family lived in exile in Stockholm.

The clippings led to a long-distance conversation with a Berkeley political scientist I knew slightly, who'd once taught with Michaelis and admired his work and ideas. That led in turn to a couple of Michaelis' essays in scholarly journals. They impressed me with their clarity of thought, but also with their compassion, their concern with the common good: all too rare among economists. There was something special about the man.

In Stockholm, evidently, Michaelis wasn't just nursing his wounds. He'd founded something called the Hellenic Socialist Liberation Movement, a vehicle to build international opposition to the junta, and was travelling a great deal, lobbying foreign governments and raising money from Greeks abroad. When he arrived in Toronto on a speaking tour, I went to hear him at the university. His speech was electrifying.

Sitting next to me in Convocation Hall was another author of mine, chairman of the political science department, who was also powerfully struck by Michaelis' address. Over whiskys at the Faculty Club afterwards, we discussed with mounting and unaccustomed excitement Michaelis' courage, his conviction, his centrality to any return to democracy in Greece. By the end of the evening, we'd come up with an idea: a guest Chair in European Political Studies. Over the ensuing weeks, my author and I persuaded the university vice-president, and together the three of us persuaded the president, to use a recent bequest to fund the Chair, and to appoint Michaelis Kastri its first occupant.

Michaelis took eagerly to the idea; Toronto was a more strategic base than Stockholm from which to lobby Washington. Persuading the university board of governors, however, was much more difficult. Those distinguished gentlemen and ladies had heard Michaelis was some sort of Red—which he

21

was, of course, if you saw the world as they did—and it was only after much cosseting and stroking that we were able to reassure them that he was a social democrat and a victim of fascism, comparable to the intellectuals persecuted by Hitler, as well as a brilliant scholar admired around the world who would attract prestige and money to the university. At last Michaelis assumed the Chair in the fall term, 1971.

The little man in Mitropolis Square never knew it, but he'd exerted an influence on his hero's fortunes. He'd also made possible one of the important relationships of my life.

Once Michaelis moved his family to their new home—a split-level country estate north of Toronto, with a swimming pool and electrified fence and Alsatian guard dogs (the Colonels were known to send hit-men after their enemies in exile) —he invited me up for a swim and dinner. I told him about seeing the arrival of his father's coffin, about being in the crowd during the funeral. Although Michaelis had heard about that day from his family, I was the first eyewitness he'd spoken to who'd mixed with the mob in the square. He listened transfixed: hungry for every last detail I could remember.

After that, Michaelis and I would dine together every couple of months. I was his connection to his adopted country, as I saw it—his land of exile, as he did.

We never became truly close. He was always far too busy building the Movement for that, flying off to Washington or New York or London to raise money and hector politicians about the junta. But we did agree that this was the time for him to write his long-planned comparative study of socialist systems in Sweden, the Soviet Union, and China, and that my firm should publish it. We signed a contract, with only a modest advance; Michaelis wasn't in great need of money. With its international rights potential, the book was quite a catch for the company.

But for me, the book was secondary. Entering the orbit of Michaelis' intelligence, his moral authority, was far more important. His warmth and largeness of spirit came to be very dear to me. This was especially so because my marriage to Una was slowly and painfully unravelling, and I needed allies badly.

After Una and I finally separated, people I'd considered good friends for years dropped me from their invitation lists, avoided me in supermarkets, froze when I called them on the telephone. A few simply blamed me for causing the breakup. Others thought they couldn't remain friends with both of us, and I was the one they sacrificed. For still others, apparently, I'd contracted a highly contagious social disease. Worse yet, I had become vice-president of the firm after the coup of acquiring Michaelis; certain colleagues began keeping their distance, resentful of my so-called "power". Of course, Michaelis felt no such squeamishness.

He represented a number of things to me — perhaps too much, I can see now. He was my professional inspiration, my intellectual touchstone, even a kind of belated mentor, although he was barely ten years older, and at my age I should have been past the point of needing mentors.

But our times together were memorable occasions. They were invariably marked by a wonderful sense of discovery— the excitement of long, exploratory conversations with a colleague who takes the trouble to challenge your preconceptions and introduce you to places you hadn't expected to go. At lunch we'd talk well into the afternoon, at dinner well into the evening. Michaelis provided me with a sense of hope, of fresh horizons, which I needed badly.

In the summer of 1974, as it became clear the junta was finally collapsing from its own inertia and stupidity, I was selfishly sorry that happy outcome would mean I'd be losing him. There would be nothing to keep Michaelis in Toronto any longer. For all I knew, I might never see him again. It was a terrible shame — not only for me, but for Nick, who had admired Michaelis almost as much as I did.

*   *   *

Finally a fragment of brown coastline emerged from the silvery sea below, like an image developing on film. The passengers craned their necks to look out the windows on the port side, calling to their neighbours to come and see, then taking another long look themselves, as if they couldn't quite believe their eyes. They turned and told each other how *orea* — beautiful — the sight was.

A debate ensued as to whether the coast was really Greece, or just Yugoslavia or Albania. The shrunken grandmother across the aisle from me had no doubts. After passing the flight in stoic silence, eyes closed, she was now weeping softly but unselfconsciously. Her white-haired husband sitting beside her turned and looked at me over the top of her head; briefly our eyes met, acknowledging each other's historical moment. I nodded to him. For him and his old woman, this journey meant a long-awaited rounding of a great circle, a hoped-for completion. They couldn't have imagined what it meant for me. I didn't know myself.

As the aircraft banked over the Saronic Gulf, and the sprawling, dirty-white smear of the capital materialized out of thick brown haze, wild cheering erupted from all parts of the cabin. A blonde flight attendant winced, covering her delicate ears. Oh Athens. It was a return for me, too, after all. I swallowed the last of my Scotch. Fingers of anxiety and longing were clawing at my insides — Nick was down there somewhere, albeit in a cell, and whatever the circumstances, I'd surely be seeing him soon, taking him into *my* custody — and I became so excited I felt like cheering too.

4

The Attic sun was like a blow to the head. I made my way down the passenger ladder among the eager jostling Greeks, and a silver and blue Olympic Airways bus whisked us in a sweltering mass, standing-room only, from the aircraft to the terminal building. Inside, it was blessedly air-conditioned. I lined up for passport control, put my navy blazer back on. Restoring the knot to my tie, I felt excessively tall and pale among the passengers shouting to friends and relatives herded behind metal barriers.

Soldiers were stationed in pairs around the terminal. Some of them cradled ugly submachine guns, others held clipboards with sheaves of papers containing God-knows-what directives and lists. Methodically they gave us all the once-over. They made me nervous. But after lengthy questioning of the returning Greeks, I was passed over with scarcely a glance. The official in the glass box stamped my passport without even examining it. I was accepted at face value: a foreigner of means, likely travelling on business, a bringer of foreign currency, certainly not a Turk. Who needed to know more than that?

My suitcase still hadn't arrived on the baggage carousel. Impatient to get into the city, I busied myself cashing a traveller's cheque for drachmas at the exchange counter, then walked over to a newsstand festooned with magazines, maps, and postcards of the Acropolis. Athens is a great city for newspapers. At least a dozen were suspended by wooden clothespegs from an overhead wire. And from every front page, like another telegram, Michaelis' face leaped out at me.

So he was back already: this both delighted and dismayed me. Surely it wasn't safe for him *yet*. The head of the

25

provisional government, Karamanlis, was his father's old nemesis, and no amnesty for political exiles had yet been declared. In such an unsettled situation, anything could happen. What guarantee was there that Michaelis would be allowed to remain free? Or safe from some assassin's bullet? None, obviously. But just as obviously, he'd accepted those risks. And at the same time, the news photographs were tremendously reassuring—as if Michaelis were welcoming me personally to his homeland, urging me on in my mission. I felt heartened, strengthened. Less alone. I had an ally after all.

I examined the newspapers more closely. The photographs captured every stage of Michaelis' progress when he'd arrived at the airport the night before, on a flight from Frankfurt: emerging from the aircraft, floodlit against the black sky; waving as he descended the ladder, joyful; taking his first steps on Greek soil in six years, reverential; proceeding through the welcoming throng in the lobby, Party officials at both elbows, a forest of arms straining towards him. In every shot, his thoughtful scholar's face was transformed into an ikon of fierce ecstasy—the thickly woven eyebrows arched in extravagant triumph. The image shocked me a little. I'd never seen Michaelis on his home ground before.

I gratified the newsvendor by buying a copy of the *Athens News*, the little English-language daily, to get the full story. The crowd that had met him at the airport was estimated at two thousand—not bad, although hardly stupendous by Greek standards. Many of his supporters were still afraid to declare themselves publicly.

Michaelis had held an impromptu press conference right there in the lobby. Even in the awkward *Athens News* translation, his rhetoric was stirring:

"Greeks will not be content to trade one autocracy for another, no matter how benevolent. As yet Mr. Karamanlis has no mandate from the people—the people who have suffered so long and painfully under the fascist regime. He will have our support only so long as he releases all citizens imprisoned for their courageous opposition to the junta, and as long as he makes haste towards free and fair elections.

"First there must be a representative assembly to frame a

democratic constitution. Then a general election for a Parliament to guarantee that constitution, free of interference from the army. As soon as Mr. Karamanlis deviates from that course, he becomes an enemy of the people."

Farther down in the story, Michaelis was quoted as saying: "The provisional government has a solemn responsibility to investigate the massacre at the Athens Polytechnic. ESA officers responsible for that terrible crime must be brought to justice, up to and including Brigadier Ioannides. All anti-democratic forces in the military, associated with the tyrants and their CIA masters, must be ruthlessly purged."

"Ruthlessly": coming from Michaelis, the word seemed extraordinary, even when applied to the ruthless military police in the ESA.

Quickly I scanned the rest of the front page. Michaelis' homecoming wasn't the only big event. The main headline was reserved for an exchange of telegrams between Karamanlis and Prime Minister Ecevit of Turkey. The leaders were busy hurling threats at each other, softened by signals of conciliation, of willingness to negotiate, provided certain "nonnegotiable" points were accepted. Cyprus remained tense. But for the moment, the ceasefire was holding.

Hold on a bit longer, just a few more days, I thought, and with luck and a little help from Michaelis, I'll get Nick out of here. I stuck the newspaper into the side pocket of my blazer, located my suitcase, and walked outside into the preposterous heat.

5

I n the cab going into the city, I wondered why I didn't feel better.

Here I was, drawing closer to Nick every moment; but the reality of Athens kept intervening, thrusting itself through the streaky windshield between me and my son with an importunate ugliness that was impossible to ignore. Once we'd left the airport behind, the dry hills dotted with stunted trees, the sea in the distance shimmering and parched, we entered a wasteland of cement and traffic. I'd forgotten how ramshackle the city was. The detritus of half-constructed apartment blocks littered the streets, thick plaster dust overlay everything. In the midst of it all, a deep-pink explosion of bougainvillea cascaded down a cement-block wall, but not far enough to mask the garbage heaped in the ditch beneath.

I tried to imagine seeing Nick in a few hours: the two of us talking, heads close together, making plans to spring him loose. Christ, what plans? I didn't have any! This wasn't like home, where I had contacts, a modicum of authority, rights that I could call upon. What was I going to do for Nick *here*? Anything, I supposed—anything would be better than nothing at all.

I wondered how different he was now, how much of the old bond between us had survived. Perhaps it took an emergency to find out. Although I knew better, I entertained the bleak thought that this whole thing would never have happened if Una and I hadn't separated: so much ill, it seemed, could be blamed on that single event.

I felt angry with myself for thinking that way—as if there were no other causal events in the universe. Even so, furtive tricks of memory kept glimmering at the edges of my vision, dancing around corners, vanishing into thin air. A pair of insatiable lovers, astonished to be discovering the anomalies of Greece together. Hiking the jagged, desiccated coastline of Ios. Plunging naked into the waters of a deserted cove on Paros. Picking purple and white anemones on a hillside in Crete. Laying in a supply of rough red wine in a wicker-covered demijohn, then enjoying it in the evenings by ourselves on a terrace high above the cobalt sea, needing no other company —

Foolish, bloody nostalgia. Its ambushes were everywhere. Willing myself back to the present, I found for a moment I was unable to remember the name of the embassy official I was so anxious to meet, whose telex to Ottawa had set this whole journey in motion: ah yes, Eleni Diamantides. Key to my hopes and plans.

I pictured her as a sensible Greek bourgeoise, perhaps with teenagers of her own, even grown-up children. She'd understand a parent's desperation. She'd be practical and efficient, entirely capable of browbeating the dull-witted cops who'd arrested my kid, of helping me prove it was all a stupid mistake, a misunderstanding. And when she'd succeeded in getting Nick placed in my custody, maybe he'd get around to explaining why in God's name he'd gone to Greece without even telling me — especially now, of all the harebrained times. What had happened to his good sense?

I scanned buildings for stigmata of change, of liberation, but the sidestreets just looked congested, the apartments shuttered against the heat. Parked cars gave the impression of being abandoned. Farther along, small shops and cafés were open for business, and pedestrians crossed the street at reckless and unpredictable angles — nothing out of the ordinary, except for a long queue outside a butcher's. I remembered some TV news footage, Athenian housewives lining up to stockpile food in case war broke out in earnest. Then I saw a large black and white poster in a café window, a portrait photograph of Karamanlis — and a moment later, another one, dogeared, taped to the rear window of a municipal bus. It showed a relatively youthful Karamanlis, middle-aged, with darker and more abundant hair than in recent photographs, so it must have been resurrected from his earlier term as prime minister.

All at once I saw what Michaelis had been driving at in his press conference. The cult of personal authority, the symbols of autocracy, still held sway—only the face had changed. Somebody had ordered that portrait to be placed in the bus; somebody else had obeyed. A dictator's portrait had been replaced, possibly even burned. What, then, was Karamanlis? I wondered if he'd ordered the removal of the junta's eavesdroppers from the telephone system. Or if he even intended to. Danger lay buried in this city like an unexploded bomb. I felt the return of the old, once-familiar mantle of paternal responsibility settling on my shoulders: no one else was going to protect Nick but me.

The traffic worsened steadily as we penetrated the downtown core. The noise was tremendous: the crashing of gears, the abrupt grinding of brakes, the nervous revving of engines. Squeezed between blue diesel buses spewing exhaust, we crawled past Hadrian's unremarkable arch, then the smashed pillars of Olympian Zeus. In the middle distance, Mount Lykabettos reared up precipitously, thrusting its tiny white chapel at the discoloured sky. Drivers honked at each other for lack of anything to do. The thick stink of diesel hung everywhere. It took us five minutes to cover the final three blocks to the Olympic Palace Hotel, where my secretary had booked me a room.

It was on Philellinon Street, just across from the old Russian church with its free-standing belltower and clutch of palm trees, and although the hotel lacked the cachet of the Grande Bretagne or the King George down the street, it was a good deal cheaper. Also, I'd never stayed there before; it wouldn't remind me too much of the past.

A bellhop showed me to a large corner room on the fifth floor. Thanks to the war scare, the hotel was practically empty —I could have had my pick of rooms. This one was air-conditioned and remarkably quiet, considering the bedlam down in the streets. Gratefully I climbed out of the damp clothes I'd been wearing since yesterday. The double bed was tempting, but it was already eleven-thirty, local time: in two hours the city would shut down for the afternoon, and I couldn't risk missing Mrs. Diamantides.

After a quick shower, I glanced in the bathroom mirror. Surprised by what I saw, I took a closer look: a long-faced, fair-haired, red-eyed northerner stared back at me, only slightly the worse for wear. He looked remarkably calm and level-headed, really, far more collected than I felt inside. Once I'd dressed him up in a white shirt and my beige summer suit (so light it weighed only a pound) and the most conservative tie I owned — navy blue, with the University of Toronto crest poised halfway down — he looked almost distinguished, a successful professional. Perhaps even a family man.

I shook myself, like someone coming out of a dream. The tie was a symbol that cut absolutely no ice in Athens. But I did feel better wearing it.

6

I hurried down Philellinon Street, to the vast quadrangle of light and noise called Constitution Square. A policeman directed the sluggish traffic pushing its way around the perimeter, under the watchful stare of multinational advertisers: SIEMENS, PAN AMERICAN, ROTHMANS, CITIBANK, OLIVETTI. Gesturing furiously, he blew his whistle without discernible effect on the drivers manoeuvring around him in mad fits and starts.

Rather than search for a free taxi in that chaos, I decided it would be faster to walk the few blocks to the embassy. I cut diagonally across the middle of the square, under blue awnings, through empty ranks of tables and chairs unoccupied by tourists, like seats for a play doomed by bad reviews. Beyond the blank, pale yellow façade of Parliament and the fancy hotels, the traffic spread out across six lanes on Vasillis Sophias Avenue. I walked alongside the National Gardens, beneath a row of wilting trees, catching a startling whiff amid the exhaust of the sharp, feminine, long-forgotten scent of jasmine.

The embassy occupied the ground floor of a modern building on a sidestreet rising up the slope of Mount Lykabettos. In the vestibule, a receptionist and her desk were positioned beside an elderly uniformed guard. The receptionist, no longer young herself, eyed me in the suspicious manner of Greek functionaries. I explained my business and, on impulse, introduced myself as Doctor Urquhart; she didn't need to know I'd never completed my thesis.

At "Doctor", her manner changed to grudging respect. She telephoned through and spoke, in Greek too rapid for me to understand, to Mrs. Diamantides herself.

They held a conversation while I stood there waiting like a supplicant. I wondered what they had to discuss at such length. Finally the receptionist hung up and told me to take a seat in the waiting room inside. I made a show of impatience, checking my watch. I would wait exactly five minutes, I decided, before insisting on seeing Mrs. Diamantides at once.

A library adjoined the waiting room, and someone had left a *Globe and Mail* scattered across the reading table, an issue I recognized from two weeks earlier. A large bulletin board covered with notices hung on the wall. Perhaps Nick had come here before his misadventure; perhaps he'd even read the notices. My spirits lifted, and I scanned the messages eagerly:

"For sale. White 1971 Renault Dauphine. Good condition, Greek plates."

"Montessori School/Ecole Montessori. Trilingual education English/French/Greek for preschoolers to grade six."

"Speak Greek in two weeks, daily lessons, telephone...."

"Canadian university student soaking up Greek culture, female, will baby- or house-sit. Reasonable rates. If interested, leave message at reception for Ms...."

"Mr. Urquhart? How do you do. I'm Helen. Eleni, they probably said."

A woman was smiling pleasantly at me. I stared: she was at least fifteen years younger than my mental image of her. Sleeveless dress, rather sporty for a diplomat, bare arms tanned a shade deeper than her face. It was a strong-featured yet pretty face, light olive in complexion, softened by natural dark curls. I experienced the usual confusion over whether you're supposed to shake a woman's hand. Will it be deemed a token of equality, or mere male forwardness? I waited for her to extend her hand, but she didn't.

"If you'll come this way, we can talk in my office," she said briskly, as if we were about to process some routine consular matter.

I fell into step alongside her swift sure stride. I wondered if she'd talked to Nick. Actually *seen* him. I wanted to blurt my questions right there in the corridor.

Eleni/Helen's office was tiny, with a window and two wing-backed chairs facing a desk. Somehow she herself didn't go with the art on her wall—a government-issue reproduction of red autumn maples beside a northern lake. I sat down in one of the chairs, crossed my legs, and folded my hands in my lap, collecting myself.

She shut the door. Seated behind her desk, she fussed with some papers before looking up. She gave me another smile, less confident this time.

"I really want to apologize," she announced in a single rushed breath.

"Apologize? Why is that?" Instinctively I adopted the manner I used with authors asking for an extension of their deadline: understanding and forbearing, but all business.

Her expression clouded. "On behalf of the embassy. No one has been to the prison yet. To visit your son."

"So I gathered."

"You knew?" She seemed relieved. "We've just been *so* busy. All our time has been taken up getting Canadians out of here. Tourists who wouldn't wait for their flights, tour operators worried about getting sued—it was crazy." Her voice was fresh, airy, like a girl's, yet her grey eyes held mine with adult directness. "When the Swedes sent planes to remove their nationals, our people demanded we do the same. Somehow we got them all out on commercial flights and trains and ferries, I don't know how. We were even renting cars for people. And now the panic's over and still nothing's happened—nothing disastrous, anyway—but we haven't had a minute to look into your son's arrest. I can't tell you how sorry I am...."

"Mrs. Diamantides—"

"And next thing we heard, you were coming in person. We just got the telex from Ottawa this morning."

"And here I am." Her concern seemed so genuine, I had to force myself to be stern with her. "Do you realize something? I still don't know why Nick was arrested."

"Oh." She looked down at the file open on her desk. "Here's the official version. Roughly translated as: 'Illegal entry at Hellinikon Airport by means of an invalid passport.'"

And she looked up quizzically at me and blinked, as if I

could explain that peculiar circumstance.

I was so startled I laughed. "But that's absurd!"

"Yes?" she said.

"Nick has a perfectly valid passport. Issued just last year. It has four more years before it expires."

"I see." She nodded slowly, thoughtfully, turning from my undocumented claim to the official version in the file:

"'Suspect retained in custody at Bouboulinas'—that's a prison, not too far from here—'pending court appearance at earliest convenience.'"

The stark, unequivocal reality—Nick held in a foreign jail, prior to being tried in a foreign court, in an alien language, under incomprehensible, undemocratic, non-Anglo-Saxon laws—formed unpleasantly in my mind.

"*Whose* convenience? How long do they plan to hold him anyway?"

She remained calm. "I wish I could tell you that. Let's see what else: 'Suspect apprehended at Hellinikon passport control. No resistance to arrest. No known companions. No plea by accused.' That's all, I'm afraid."

"No plea? That doesn't sound like Nick—he'd be pleading not guilty, demanding his rights—demanding to see you people, at the very least...."

"Maybe he did. Maybe it's the language barrier. He could be disoriented, not knowing if he *has* any rights. He's probably a little freaked out."

"Didn't he ask to send a telegram home? Or anything?"

"Possibly. The embassy has to be informed in these cases anyway. And you're listed in Nick's passport as the person to be notified in case of emergency. That's how we knew to inform you."

Unexpectedly, a silence fell between me and this well-meaning young woman—a parenthesis composed of mutual awkwardness and confusion. The more I learned, it seemed, the less I understood. Finally I remembered to say the things I'd been rehearsing and revising all the way across the Atlantic and half of Europe.

"Mrs. Diamantides, there's something I want to make clear to you."

She stirred uncomfortably in her chair. But all she said was, "Call me Helen, okay?"

I nodded and tried to smile. "Helen, I don't know what Nick has done, exactly, to get himself into this. But I want him out of here. I want that very badly. I've come to do whatever's needed, post bail, pay fines, court fees, bribes, whatever. And I'm prepared to stay as long as necessary. I'll take Nick into my custody. I'll be responsible for him — the authorities can be assured of that."

I waited for this to sink in before continuing. "I have a — a substantial sum of money with me, entirely for obtaining Nick's release. I can get more if necessary. The Athens branch of the Bank of Nova Scotia has instructions to release funds on my signature. In Greek currency. You never know, maybe the court doesn't accept traveller's cheques."

She smiled at my poor joke. I pulled the plane ticket out of my breast pocket, obtained with the help of an old classmate who was now an executive with the airline: "This is an open ticket to fly Nick home. It's all ready to go." I was surprised to hear a catch in my voice. "Would you mind putting all this on the record, please? Helen? I want the ambassador to be fully informed of the situation."

"Of course." She made some quick notes with a ballpoint pen. "Unfortunately, Ambassador Gordon has had to go into hospital. A small emergency, nothing too serious. I'll see he's briefed as soon as he returns."

"He picked a hell of a time," I said, an ungracious remark that Helen was tactful enough to ignore. "Sorry. I was just hoping he'd put his weight behind the case. Lean on the authorities a bit."

"Well, he'll *try*. Insofar as it's possible." Then she said, "It might help if you could tell me more about Nick. What was he doing in Greece exactly, before... *this* happened?"

I felt uncomfortable to be asked, and it probably showed, but I owed her some kind of explanation. "I'm afraid I don't have a whole lot of details. I assume he's been touring around — seeing the sights, getting to know the culture. Same as he's been doing in other countries. He's been in Europe nearly a year."

"Ah—so he's taken time off to travel."

"Exactly."

"Sort of a post-grad year?"

"Sort of. Except he hasn't graduated yet. He did exceptionally well in high school—first in his class, basketball captain, school debater, all that sort of thing. He did so much it was a little freakish, to tell you the truth. But life fell apart for him at college."

"Oh?"

I didn't really want to get into this, but now that I'd started, I had to go on. "Two things, I guess. He'd been deeply involved with his girlfriend in high school. Lovely girl, intelligent, spirited...they were inseparable. They were going to move away to university together. Then she changed her mind. Decided she wanted to wait a year, and work for a social agency instead. So Nick went on without her. He hoped they'd stay close by writing and phoning and so on, meeting for weekends. It didn't happen. She got involved with an older man. That really threw him. He barely passed his year."

"I see. And the other thing?"

"Well, it's harder to prove the impact of this one. I know it affected him, naturally, but he's never really told me. His mother and I separated—about two years ago. Just before he left for college. I'm sure that played its part."

"In what? Pardon me for asking—I don't want to pry. I'm just trying to form a picture of your son."

"Of course. I think our separation made him very... critical of the world. Maybe cynical is a better word. He lost faith in a lot of things. Even his activism. He'd been a great peace worker."

"Did he drop out?"

"Not permanently. He wanted to—he insisted his courses weren't relevant any more to what he wanted to be. Whatever that was."

"Sounds like he was confused."

"Yes. Off balance. The only thing he seemed positive about was travel. So finally, he made a deal with his mother and me: he'd work for the summer, then the three of us would each finance one-third of his year in Europe. I agreed on condition that he return to university in September."

"That's next month," Helen observed.

"Indeed. Seems like he'll be taking his degree by correspondence from jail."

She almost allowed herself to laugh, then turned to her telephone, pausing rather solemnly, I thought, before dialing a single digit. She murmured into the mouthpiece, "John? Mr. Urquhart is here. Shall we go to your office? Or do you want to come in here?"

I felt upset about having to expose my private life. And irrationally, I resented the idea of somebody else barging in on our discussion so soon. But in a moment there was a brisk rap on the door, and I told myself not to be foolish — this other official, this John, might be in a position to help.

Walking in with hand already extended, he wasn't much older than Helen, and like everyone else in this climate he was bare-armed, wearing a white shortsleeved shirt and dark blue old-boy's tie: McGill. With his cleanly parted, short dark hair, symmetrical features, and white smile, he looked the perfect young diplomat.

"Mr. Urquhart," he said as we shook hands. He said it "Erk-ew-art" instead of "Erk-urt", as it's meant to be pronounced. "Delighted to meet you. John Ferrier, second secretary and vice-consul."

As I sat down, I noticed John Ferrier was a little thick around the middle, not perfect after all. He perched on the corner of Helen's desk as if he owned it, looking covetously down on her. She seemed to shrink backwards slightly, removing herself from the proceedings.

He said, "I assume Helen's filled you in."

"Yes. And I have to say, I'm at a loss. This charge makes no sense to me at all. What do you make of it?"

Ferrier lifted his eyebrows, sighed, and shook his head, gestures of helplessness over the folly of others. "To be perfectly frank, sir, nothing that happens in Greece surprises me. I suppose we'll just have to see what the authorities can tell us."

"Exactly. So I'd like to visit them right away. I need to

see Nick, make sure he's being treated properly. But I also want to meet these authorities face to face—let them know what they're dealing with. I've been explaining to Helen how urgent it is to get Nick out of here, and—"

"Mr. Urquhart has funds with him," she put in softly. "For posting bail."

Ferrier seemed thrown off stride, unprepared for a call to action quite so soon, but he recovered at once.

"I'm glad you were able to come in person, sir. Your presence could be invaluable, only I must warn you: nothing *ever* happens quickly in Greece. Especially where officialdom is involved. Sorting out this mess could take days, weeks— months, even. Hate to say that, but I think it's best to warn you now, so you won't be disappointed later."

Ferrier's heartiness, his forced solicitude, grated on me. Helen, edging back still farther in her chair, seemed to understand this.

"Then we'd better get started," I told him. "I want to leave for the prison. Immediately, if you don't mind."

He gave a condescending little laugh. "I'm not sure they'd be willing to see us on such short notice, sir. Or even see us at all. In any case, it's almost lunchtime."

"Mr. Ferrier, I don't care if it's lunchtime, I've just flown five thousand miles for this meeting."

"Yes, sir. Well, it's worth a try," he said, clearly disbelieving this. "Of course we'll have to phone ahead. No doubt they'll make us cool our heels while they consider our request."

I turned to Helen. "Will you come too?" I asked.

Resuming his air of decisiveness, Ferrier thrust himself off her desk. "Oh, that wouldn't be advisable, sir. All men at Bouboulinas. No place for a woman. Is it, Helen?"

I continued sitting in her office while Ferrier went off to make the phone call. Suddenly Helen and I had nothing further to say to each other. The tension between those two had been like ground glass, and she didn't like me witnessing it. The encounter had changed her entire manner. She took a nervous swipe at a stray lock of hair, her eyebrows tightened into a peevish scowl, and I decided to leave her alone while she busied herself with her papers. For distraction, I stared at the red Canadian maples beside the empty Canadian lake, as if some concealed animal might burst from those woods at any moment.

In a few minutes Ferrier returned, looking sheepish. "I don't understand it," he said. "It's quite unusual. They actually seem anxious to meet you."

Helen recovered a glimmer of a smile as we left, signalling silently to me with fingers crossed.

7

I followed John Ferrier out a side entrance and across the street, to a row of parked cars facing the curb. He un-locked a somber black Peugeot with diplomatic plates. The car wasn't air-conditioned, so even with the windows down it was broiling inside.

We drove along a couple of tree-lined sidestreets, then entered the traffic on Vasillis Sophias, past the glass and marble crescent of the Athens Hilton. In '68, I'd taken Nick swimming in the famous Hilton pool, curious to know why it was so popular with middle-class Athenians. Now a simple everyday act like going for a swim, even riding in a car, was forbidden him. All my unanswered questions closed in: How much longer would he have to stay in jail? What was it doing to his spirit? His health? Were they feeding him adequately? What kind of people was he locked up with? I was about to get answers.

Suddenly I felt excited again, eager for the sight of him. I could practically feel the two of us hugging, laughing in relief. At the same time, I realized I'd better prepare myself for the worst — the reality of him behind bars — and accept it, for the moment, with as much equanimity as I could. If he saw me behaving as upset as I felt, it would just lower his morale.

I forced myself to consider the possibility that Nick *had* committed some offence — had in fact lost his passport, or done some other foolish, incomprehensible thing with it. I had to be ready for that, too: ready for anything. All that really mattered for the moment was ensuring he was all right.

I'd scarcely glanced at the buildings we were passing on the wide avenue, or at stolid John Ferrier behind the wheel, but now I focused on him. I knew he was annoyed with me for forcing him into this trip, spoiling his lunch break; no doubt he had better things to do than visit prisons. Still, he'd become crucial to my purpose. He was the one with fluency in Greek and, I hoped, some clout with the local authorities. If I had to rely on him instead of Helen, I'd better try to win him over to Nick's cause. I wouldn't even correct his pronunciation of my surname, or tell him to stop calling me "sir".

"Mr. Ferrier," I said to his right ear. "Any children of your own?"

"Afraid not, sir," he answered, keeping his eyes on the traffic. "Not married. Not yet, anyway."

"Can I tell you something? I hope you don't mind. It's apropos of Nick."

"Go ahead, sir," he said. "Please."

"Well—basically, it's just that being a parent never quite ends. Even after your kid grows up, you still worry sometimes. How is he managing, can he handle himself in the world, stuff like that. You've got into the habit. You can't live his life for him of course, you don't even want to, but you don't stop feeling responsible to some extent. That's why I'm here. Nick already has two strikes against him. He doesn't speak the language, and the country might go to war any minute."

"That's certainly true." Ferrier pursed his lips, and I imagined I could feel him straining to take in what I'd said, to empathize a little, not being sure how to express it.

Finally he said, "Please excuse me for asking. But is your son a drug-user? Not the hard stuff, of course. Marijuana? Hash? Kif?"

This startled me. I hadn't seriously considered drugs as the cause of Nick's problem. At the same time, I knew I couldn't answer the question with any certainty. What did I know about my son's private pastimes—even at university, much less during his year abroad? I wasn't sure I wanted to know.

"I guess I've kind of assumed he's tried some grass," I said. "Don't they all? Beyond that—"

"Ninety per cent of these cases involve dope," Ferrier

replied with absolute finality. "Nationality doesn't matter. American, British, Australian, Canadian, these kids all think they can get away with it. They're so far from home, they figure no more limits. They don't realize how seriously governments take drugs in this part of the world. Even possession, just a few grams. So they end up in deep trouble. Dreadful prisons. The sentences can be terribly harsh."

I tried to assess this possibility. "But if drugs are the problem, why doesn't it say so in your dossier? Why all this stuff about a false passport?"

He shrugged. "Just a hunch. We'll see. The Greek authorities aren't always as straightforward as we'd like."

We turned a corner, passing a huge Stars and Stripes hanging behind a spiked metal fence surrounding the U.S. embassy, then around another corner. We'd reached a residential quarter of gracious white villas. The one conspicuous exception was a big, institutional structure hunched behind a wall hedged with acacia trees, their few pale blossoms drooping in the heat.

Turning into an opening in the wall, we were waved through by two helmeted soldiers, automatic rifles slung over their shoulders, who bent down to check our diplomatic plates. One of them wrote the number on a clipboard. More soldiers were stationed at the entrance to the building. The plaque on the wall did not say "Bouboulinas".

Something clicked into place. "Isn't this the *military* prison?" I asked Ferrier. "ESA headquarters? Brigadier Ioannides, and all that?"

"You know a lot about Greece, sir."

"Please stop calling me that. Some friends of mine are Greek. You didn't tell me we were coming here."

A sentry gestured to us to get out.

"Apparently your son was transferred here this morning. They told me over the phone just now. I didn't want to alarm you."

"But why?"

"Something about jurisdiction. Ever since the coup, the ESA has authority over the airport."

"But the junta's finished now."

43

"Yes sir. I'm not sure how much difference that really makes."

The sentry stood waiting beside Ferrier's door, while another soldier opened the door on my side. I ignored them. A trifle pedantically, I said, "Let me remind you, it was Ioannides who had those kids massacred at the Polytechnic. And *he's* not in jail."

*　*　*

The moment I stepped out of the car, I felt a clenching in the pit of my stomach, an unpleasant tightening in my bowels. It was the unfamiliar onset of plain fear — as if I were the one about to be imprisoned.

One of the sentries got behind the wheel of our car and drove it away somewhere, leaving Ferrier and me exposed out in the open. Another soldier examined Ferrier's diplomatic credentials, then made a brusque report into a two-way radio, answered by another voice crackling an acknowledgement.

A young uniformed officer emerged from the prison entrance. He descended the steps, looking almost civilian because he was wearing neither a helmet nor a gun, and blinked rapidly against the sunlight as he looked enquiringly at the two of us. Ferrier stated our business in Greek. The officer nodded and turned to escort us inside: we were expected.

I'd never imagined that one day I'd enter a fascist prison. The corridors were dim and dreary, heavy with the reek of some ammonia disinfectant. The walls, once painted lime-green, were discoloured to a queasy brown by cigarette smoke. A greasy wooden moulding ran the length of the walls at elbow-height. I felt deeply, fundamentally angry to think they had Nick in there.

The officer showed Ferrier and me to an office containing a roll-top wooden desk and two chairs upholstered in cracked brown leather, placed at right angles to one another. No window. The door, encasing a pane of frosted glass, closed behind us. I glanced at Ferrier. He looked as if he didn't like being there any more than I did.

For a moment I had the comforting illusion of being in a principal's office, awaiting a report on my son's misdemeanours at school. Once, Nick had written an off-colour political satire for his highschool drama group, which the principal had considered subversive and obscene, and I'd been called in to discuss it. If only the offence were so trivial this time! The illusion dissolved at the sight of the blue and white flag standing limply in the corner, the choked ashtray overflowing onto some papers alongside a goose-necked metal lamp and a demitasse of cold coffee.

"Pleasant, isn't it?" Ferrier said. Even he seemed nervous.

"Who are we supposed to see?"

"A Major Christos Drakonakis. The commanding officer."

"Will he let me visit Nick?" Previously, I'd just assumed that's why we were there; now I wasn't so sure.

"We can ask."

We sat in silence in those uncomfortable chairs, in the stale unhealthy air, and every minute felt like an hour. When Major Drakonakis finally arrived, Ferrier stood reflexively, and I did the same.

The major's uniform sported the predictable quantity of braid; he wore the predictable amber-tinted sunglasses; but the gold frames gave him a strangely intellectual air. Another deviation from type was that he lacked a military moustache. His bushy eyebrows reminded me incongruously of Michaelis, and the major furthered the comparison by speaking surprisingly fluent, American-accented English, cut with a smoker's rasp.

"Good morning gentlemen!" He hurled the words at us like an order. "Or is it afternoon? My God, I'm falling behind. How are you?"

Major Drakonakis gave off a blend of cigarette smoke and aftershave. He squeezed and pumped our hands in turn, seeming to know instantly which of us was the diplomat and which the father of the wayward child—acting, in fact, as if he'd known us both for years. He offered an imitation smile, a pro-forma baring of teeth stained yellow with nicotine.

The closely shaven cheeks and high forehead were gleaming and impenetrable.

"Take a seat," he boomed.

I sank back once more onto the brittle surface of the chair, but Ferrier remained on his feet and jumped in without formalities.

"Major, Mr. Urquhart here has come all the way from Canada to see his son. He's concerned—"

"Upset," I interjected.

"—and upset that his son has been incarcerated. He wishes to arrange for Nicholas to be released into his custody. He is prepared to deposit bail money and to pay whatever costs are in order. Could you tell us, please, if this is possible?"

"Quite right," I added quickly, looking up at Drakonakis from my chair, a maddeningly inferior position. I pulled out the airline folder: "Major, I'll take responsibility for Nicholas. I'll personally guarantee he'll appear in court. Or simply leave the country, if you prefer. At once. On this airline ticket."

This short speech left me sweating and shaky.

Ferrier sat down. The major, however, remained standing, looming above us, visibly unmoved. He turned to his desk and extracted a manila file folder from the clutter.

"Of course. If I were in your shoes, mister, I'd feel exactly the same way."

I waited for him to open the file, Nick's file, but he merely exhaled in a sudden access of weariness and impatience, gazing at the blank wall as if looking for a window that wasn't there. Did he consider our meeting a mere waste of his time after all? He reached inside the jacket of his uniform and found a crumpled package. Tilting it sideways, he shook it and ejected a filterless cigarette, which he inserted between his lips and lit with a Bic lighter, all in the practised motion of one hand. Meanwhile he continued holding the file in his other hand, not even looking at it. As the smell of strong Greek tobacco filled the room, I had an urge to snatch the file away from him, to denounce and discredit its contents. I was too jumpy to wait for Ferrier's next intervention.

"Major," I said, "I'm really very puzzled by the charge against Nicholas."

Drakonakis sat down in the swivel chair in front of his desk, lowering himself onto it slowly, as though to protect something delicate in his back. Instead of answering my question, he sucked another hard pull from his cigarette. "You have a photograph of your son with you? A recent one?"

"Yes. But you've seen it already—it's a copy of the one in his passport."

"Let me see."

As I removed the small photograph from a plastic window in my wallet, Nick's serious, intelligent eyes looked up at me through his hornrimmed glasses, warning me not to do this. With superstitious reluctance, I handed his image to the major.

Drakonakis examined the photograph. He held it up to the light of his desklamp, then raised his eyebrows and squinted at me through the smoke and amber-tinted glasses.

"Never seen it before."

"I beg your pardon? You haven't seen the passport?"

"Oh yeah, it's in the file." The major started to hand the photograph back to me—a piece of flawed merchandise—then changed his mind and dropped it into the file folder, where it would disappear from my possession for ever. "I have to keep this for our records."

"Just a second," I said. "Are you saying that's not a picture of Nick?"

"I'm saying it's not the photograph in his passport." Staring fixedly at me, Drakonakis shrugged lightly, as if the matter were scarcely worth discussing.

"But how can that be?"

Before I could dispute any further, Ferrier intervened. "Major? May I make a suggestion? Perhaps you'd allow us to visit the prisoner."

To my immense relief, Drakonakis nodded and said offhandedly, "Of course."

*   *   *

47

The three of us followed a military policeman with a holster on his hip down more corridors of deadly odours: old tobacco, stale sweat, bad plumbing. I wondered why the policeman wore a helmet inside the building. We climbed some stairs to a steel-barred partition sealing off the upper floor, where a guard standing on the other side saluted, unlocked the partition, and stepped aside to let us pass.

Drakonakis stopped to question the guard peremptorily. We had to wait while the man radioed to someone. In a minute another officer joined us, a hard-looking character with a black brushcut, who didn't salute, and whom Drakonakis didn't introduce. We all carried on together, entering yet another corridor, even more dimly lit.

My intestinal cramp returned. Already nauseated with apprehension, I gagged unexpectedly. The ammonia smell was overpowering here; I realized it wasn't disinfectant but urine, mixed with the raw stench of excrement.

The block was silent except for our echoing footsteps on the concrete floor. We passed a succession of barred cells. Although they were unlighted, I saw each one contained a prisoner, occasionally two, half hidden in the shadows, stirring anxiously as we passed. I didn't look at them. It seemed wrong to stare at human beings caged up like animals in a zoo. But then it occurred to me I *should* look at them, perhaps they needed recognition from a human face, especially one from outside this hellhole, perhaps they knew Nick, had spoken with him, shared helpful information—

Our procession stopped abruptly at the very end of the row. I felt a strange ambivalence. Desperate to talk to Nick, I was nevertheless afraid to see him locked up, inhabiting this wretched place. Then a stranger thought came: there was a kind of safety for him here, behind these bars, a protection from adversity, from the dangers of the chaotic world about to explode outside....

At the major's gestured invitation, I peered between the bars, into the recessed shadows.

Showing Nick my face, I tried to smile reassuringly. I could scarcely make out his long body reclining on a cot at the back. Was he asleep? I wondered if he'd been told I was coming, and was about to call something in a cheerful voice when Drakonakis barked like a parade-ground sergeant: "Prisoner, step forward!"

Nick hesitated. Then, visibly gathering his strength, he rose slowly from his cot and shuffled towards us, like an old man.

I was shocked, horrified. Such pained movements! I'd expected him to rush forward when he saw me.

I watched in growing alarm as the tall, angular form emerged into the brownish light from the corridor. Blue jeans and a very soiled white shirt—street clothes, not prison garb. With a new understanding, a bizarre objectivity from which emotion almost vanished, I studied the tousled black hair and aquiline nose, the handsome, sculpted mouth above a chin covered with black bristles, of a total stranger.

*   *   *

He appeared to be in his mid-twenties. Not only was he visibly older than Nick, there was really no resemblance at all, apart from height and eye colour. He wasn't even wearing glasses. His hair was much too dark. He had sallow skin, an almost feminine beauty, but at the moment his looks were seriously marred.

A purplish welt stood out below his right eye, and a corner of his mouth was cut, a sliver of a scab turning dark brown. Eyeing Drakonakis with fear and contempt—it was hard to say which predominated—he moistened the cut with the tip of his tongue. Clearly things had gone very badly for him. He knew they were only going to get worse: he tried to hang back in the centre of his cell, to protect himself with space.

Drakonakis shouted, *"Ella etho!"* and immediately the prisoner shuffled closer to us, keeping his eyes on the major and the other officer through the bars, ignoring me and Ferrier altogether.

"I don't need to say any more," Drakonakis muttered to

49

no one in particular. He turned aside to give orders to the other officer, who nodded vigorously and answered, *"Maliste."*

I stepped closer to the bars, pressing into them until I could feel the cold steel through my pant leg. I studied the battered, dirty face, committing it to memory.

"Who are you?" I asked in a peculiarly low voice, which seemed to come from someone else. "Who? Eh? Tell me. *Pios iste?*"

The prisoner looked startled, hearing even these two words in Greek from some foreign stranger. He didn't reply, but I'd thrown him sufficiently off guard that he wasn't prepared when I lunged between the bars and grabbed his shirt collar, hanging on for dear life.

"Where's Nick?" I cried uncontrollably into his face. "Where's my son? What are you doing with his passport, you bastard?"

His lips parted, his features sagged in confusion. He averted his eyes in something like anguish, then pulled away from me as hard as he could, sharply contorting his entire body sideways so that his shirt ripped loudly as he collapsed onto his knees. I looked down; I was holding his grubby torn collar in my hand.

When I looked back to the prisoner, straight into the frightened, liquid eyes, I could see behind his impostor's mask Nick's own brown eyes, looking beseechingly up at me. Imploring me to stay. To help. To forgive.

8

S afely back behind the frosted glass in the major's office, I acted unnaturally calm. Deceptively clear-headed. Since I couldn't ask the one question to which there was, apparently, still no answer, the question that kept screaming out inside my head, I distracted myself by asking Drakonakis what he knew about the prisoner. It wasn't much.

"He simply refuses to talk," Drakonakis said. "He's a very stubborn young man. A very difficult case."

It seemed the prisoner had divulged nothing whatsoever: nothing about why he'd stolen Nick's passport, or when, or where, or—the most crucial thing of all—how. He hadn't even admitted whether he'd ever *seen* Nick. Or whether he'd taken the passport by stealth, or by force.

All I knew for certain was that, in some city or town, in some country, Nick was without his passport. An awkward situation, at best. *And what else? What else?*

Ferrier and I waited while Drakonakis spoke to an underling on the telephone.

"The prisoner will break soon," the major told us confidently when he hung up. "He can't avoid talking for ever. It won't be long."

Break? Dimly I understood that this had something to do with the officer with the brushcut. In my mind's eye I saw again the prisoner's face, the beautiful, terrified eyes, and I did not feel good.

"What if there's been a mixup?" I said hurriedly, knowing how adept Greek bureaucracy is at screwing things up. "What if your men transferred the wrong prisoner this morning? Maybe Nick's still back in Bouboulinas. He doesn't speak Greek, you know," I rushed on, "there could easily have been some misunderstanding and he wouldn't know it. Wouldn't be able to set them straight—"

"There was no mistake," Drakonakis said.

"How do you know?"

"When that prisoner was arrested at the airport the other day, he was carrying this."

He reached into his file folder and held up a navy blue passport stamped "CANADA" in gold. Unceremoniously, he dropped it into my lap.

All passports look alike on the outside; yet this one projected an uncanny familiarity. It spoke to me, conveying an indefinable sense of being the very one I'd collected for Nick at the downtown passport office in Toronto eleven months earlier—and of being warmed, until recently, by contact with Nick's chest.

Opening it, I read page two:

Description of Bearer
Name: Nicholas Alan Urquhart
Birthdate: 6 Feb 1954
Birthplace: Toronto, Canada
Height: 6 Feet 2 Inches
Hair: Light Brown
Eyes: Brown
Passport Issued At: Toronto, 9 Sept 1973

All the data were accurate. But the photograph on page three, signed "Nicholas Urquhart" across the bottom in an unfamiliar, lumpy hand, was a poorly focused snapshot of the prisoner upstairs.

First I felt furious. Then weak with helplessness, with adrenalin that I was powerless to translate into action.

"That is all the evidence," Drakonakis said, withdrawing the passport from my grasp, my spirits sinking further as I felt the cover slipping between my fingertips. "Obviously the prisoner is Greek. Surely he didn't expect to get away with this *ridiculous* impersonation."

John Ferrier, whom I'd forgotten about completely, asked a question: "What's his real name?"

"Antonopoulos. Yannis Antonopoulos. He was identified by our airport security personnel—the moment he stepped off the plane. He's been wanted for some time. On other charges."

"What charges?" I asked.

Drakonakis ignored my question. It was easy for him: he was in charge. "Unfortunately, our foreign liaison branch didn't relay the complete facts to your embassy, Mr. Ferrier. The next thing we know, here is Mr. Urquhart, assuming the prisoner is his son." The major made an attempt to smile apologetically in my direction. He hadn't had much practice smiling. Or apologizing.

Presumably my presence held no further interest for him, now that I'd provided corroborating evidence that the prisoner was an impostor. The ESA had done its bureaucratic and diplomatic duty. Now he'd have liked me to kindly bugger off and leave him alone, and Nick's fate, whatever it turned out to be, would become at most a footnote to his file some day.

But I was wrong. Drakonakis began thumbing through Nick's passport, with the weary but dogged manner of someone about to deliver a lesson for someone else's benefit. He reached the page he was looking for.

"Let us see what the passport tells us," he said like a schoolmaster. "Here is an entry stamp. Athens, Hellinikon Airport, 19 July 1974. Here is also an exit stamp. Also Athens, only two days later: 21 July. Now a return to Athens: 3 August, the day the prisoner was arrested. You see?"

The major held the passport open for me, and I stared at a chaotic collage of stamped black rectangles and triangles, the documentation of Nick's travels, superimposed one on top of the other. Or was it the prisoner's travels?

"Good Lord," I said. "Into Athens — out of Athens — then back again."

"Exactly. So the prisoner could have stolen the passport between *any* of these journeys. There is no way of knowing exactly when. Or when the false photograph was inserted."

"The last time I heard from Nick," I said, "he was in Rome."

"Rome. Good. Of course. The exit stamp for 19 July says 'Roma'." Drakonakis stabbed a callused, yellowed finger at one Rome exit stamp, then at another—the departure for Athens on the third of August, which had resulted in the prisoner's arrest.

I sank back against the chair. I was in some pain—short of breath, tight chest, pounding head. "But how many of these trips did *Nick* take?"

"Perhaps none," said Ferrier, echoing my own fear.

"He could never have afforded to fly back and forth like that," I said. "He—he's not a, a businessman, he's a student, for God's sake—travelling on a shoestring."

"Shoestring?" Drakonakis wasn't sure he got it. "You mean he didn't have the money?"

"Of course not."

"Then, Mr. Urquhart," Drakonakis said more softly, a note almost of compassion entering his voice, "would you swear you have no idea if your son made *any* of these journeys?"

"I don't even know if he ever left Rome," I said dully.

The major nodded abruptly—at Ferrier, not me—and stood up. Ferrier also stood, slowly but resignedly. Our interview was over.

"So what will you do now?" I asked the major in mounting desperation. "What's the next step?"

"Next step?" He thought for a minute. "All right. We will circulate a missing-person description to Asfalia, our national security police. If your son is anywhere in Greece, they will find him. We will keep your embassy informed of any developments."

That would be a cold day in hell, I suspected. Yet, as Drakonakis shook my hand with unnecessary force, then Ferrier's, I allowed myself to hope this representative of a military dictatorship might really do what he'd said—might actually make some serious effort to find my lost boy. How could he fail to try?

9

As Ferrier and I drove back to the embassy, I lined up the facts in my mind as best I could. I tried to assemble them, like good little soldiers, into a causal pattern, but contrarily they kept tripping over one another. Even the departures and arrivals stamped in Nick's passport proved nothing. They told me where the passport had been—but not Nick. Not at all.

Against reason, I struggled to accept the situation as reasonable, capable of some rational explanation once further facts came to light. Probably it would only be a matter of time before the puzzle resolved itself like a blurred transparency snapping into focus. I tried to relax my conscious mind. Maybe some intuition would sneak up on me, some insight from the unconscious, pointing me in the right direction, towards a constructive course of action.

Yet it all kept coming back to that bruised, scared young man in the cell. *He* was the one with the answers—if only they could be pried out of him. Guiltily, I found myself hoping Drakonakis and his men were skilled and subtle interrogators, not merely sadistic goons.

"Mr. Ferrier," I said finally, "I realize this is hindsight, but we should have pressed that son of a bitch. I'm sure he knows more about the prisoner than he lets on."

"I'm afraid it wouldn't have done much good, sir. A man like that, in a country like this—he's under no obligation to reveal anything. We were lucky to even get in to see him."

I grunted. I didn't feel lucky. "Do you think he'll really have the Security Police search for Nick?"

"Possibly."

"You don't sound very hopeful."

"Sorry. I guess I'm trying to be realistic."

"Anyway, it may not matter. I'm practically certain Nick isn't in Greece."

"Oh? Why is that?"

"He's been here before. He wanted to see the *rest* of Europe. We know he was in Italy—it's my bet he still is."

Ferrier nodded slowly, resistingly, concentrating on the traffic. "In that case, I'm surprised he hasn't reported his passport stolen there."

"Maybe he has. Have you checked?"

"That's a point."

"So we still have work to do." My pulse quickened, I began to feel more hopeful. "When we get back, I'd like you to telex the embassy in Rome. Ask if they have any record of Nick or his whereabouts. Maybe he checked in there for mail, left a forwarding address or something."

"Isn't that unlikely?"

"Travellers do that sometimes."

"Yes, usually seniors or middle-aged tourists—not hippies backpacking around the Continent."

I ignored the intended slur. "I still want you to enquire. In fact, I'd like you to try all our posts in Italy, wherever we have a consulate. They should be able to reply by the end of the day. Shouldn't they?"

*   *   *

Ferrier parked the car in his reserved space in front of the embassy. To admit us, he pressed a buzzer by the main entrance; it was after two now, and the building was closed to the public.

Inside, a different receptionist sat by the phone, her little coffee cup in front of her. Looking startled by our arrival, she spoke to Ferrier in Greek: apparently something urgent. He looked quickly at me, with a directness, an interest, he hadn't shown before. The sudden narrowing of his eyes made me uncomfortable.

56

"Helen wants to see us right away," he said.

She was standing by the window in her little office, staring outside, her arms folded across her chest as if she were cold; yet the building was formidably hot, despite the air conditioning. When she turned and saw me, her features tightened.

She paused. "There's been a call. From Major Drakonakis. Mr. Urquhart, I don't know how to tell you this.... The prisoner confessed a few minutes ago."

"But that's *good*. To what?"

"Killing your son."

*   *   *

For an endless time, I couldn't think. Couldn't seem to move. Very, very slowly I sat down, into a chair Helen shoved beneath me.

Briefly, I thought I might be physically ill. Then my physical being contracted to some remote point deep inside of me. The room, the people in it, receded, until they were impossibly far away. A rushing sound filled my ears, like a massive waterfall, drowning out everything except the intake and outlet of breath.

I thought I felt my face going numb down one side. The numbness spread across my chin, my lips, all the way up the other cheekbone. With an index finger and thumb, I squeezed against my mouth to ensure it was still there. I wanted to keep reaching downwards, plunging my whole arm down my throat until I could grasp stomach and intestine and bowels and tear them out one by one.

I heard myself get out a few hoarse syllables: "What else did he say?"

"Only that. He didn't give any details." Helen was staring fixedly at me. She looked like someone who wanted to cry but couldn't. It occurred to me she was in a state of shock.

"I can't believe this," Ferrier seemed to say.

"Oh God!" Helen cried, reaching a hand towards me,

then stopping herself and thrusting it behind her back.

I felt my face again. It hadn't disintegrated after all. Time passed. People left and re-entered the room, the space my body occupied.

At some point, I began to talk. It was barely above a whisper at first, but I was definitely talking, talking to keep my head above the blackness that had opened up below me.

"Of course it's a lie," I said.

"I beg your pardon?"

"Obviously a lie," I repeated. "That boy in the cell, he's no murderer. He couldn't. Couldn't kill. Not capable of it."

"I see," Ferrier commented. He was wriggling in his chair, desperate to be elsewhere.

"I could tell from his eyes," I said.

They looked at each other. I knew what they were thinking, but they were wrong. The sunlight was too bright, the colours in the red-maple painting too vivid, the hunger in my heart too vast and all-consuming, for Nick to be dead.

"He doesn't have the hardness," I said. "Those eyes of his—they were eloquent. They told the truth. Even if he's saying the opposite."

Those twin pools of deep, flickering sadness. I could see them still, even as I became so dizzy I thought I was going to pass out. I could drown in them. *I'm not what I claim*, the eyes assured me unequivocally, *I'm only pretending. Your son is alive. Alive.*

* * *

Fortified for a moment, I was able to conduct a semblance of a conversation. Helen joined in gratefully, taking me seriously, or at least making a good show of it, eager for something to do, engaging me with practical considerations. Ferrier slumped in his chair, chewing his knuckle.

"Assuming you're right—" she said.

"Yes?" I prompted.

"Then where do you think Nick's most likely to be?"

"The prisoner—what's his name again?—"

"Antonopoulos," Ferrier said.

"Antonopoulos obtained the passport in Rome, didn't he. That's practically certain. He flew with the passport from Rome to Athens, then got arrested here, so he must have obtained it *there*. Therefore Nick is still in Italy. Maybe he's even reported the passport missing and you haven't been informed."

"Stolen passports get listed, and the list is circulated to all posts. It's automatic," Ferrier said.

"I suppose we might have missed it," Helen offered gamely. "Or Nick's name got dropped off the list somehow. Computer error, clerical mistake—it happens sometimes."

"Right," I said. "So we need to conduct a search in both countries. Greece *and* Italy. Can I count on you to organize that? An all-out search? A manhunt?"

Neither of them wanted to say anything, to commit scarce or even nonexistent resources to a hopeless cause. Their hesitation sent terrible doubt and anxiety screaming through me. I couldn't stand defeatism right then.

"I mean, what do we have to lose?" I practically shouted.

Helen dutifully waited for Ferrier to respond, but he declined.

"Our best hope might be Interpol," she suggested finally.

"We'd need the ambassador's approval," he told her.

"When's he getting back?" I asked. I was struggling to keep my voice level.

Ferrier shrugged. "Day after tomorrow. At the earliest."

"That's too long to wait," I said. "Please phone him at the hospital. Tell him what's happened." Would that help? I had no idea. I only knew we had to try everything.

"All right," Helen said. "What else would you like us to do?"

"Drakonakis said he'd have the Security Police do a search. Can we trust him to follow through?"

Ferrier frowned. "He hasn't much incentive, now."

"Couldn't you serve him with some sort of official request?"

"Certainly. We'll just keep after him," Helen said. "Insist

in the interests of international co-operation, then enquire every day how the search is going—where they're looking, what leads do they have."

"I'd like you to get the Tourist Police looking too. If Nick's in Greece, they'll find him more quickly than anybody. He stayed in youth hostels a lot."

Helen was jotting notes on her pad. "I'll ask them to check all the hostels. Same with hotel registration cards—there aren't so many of them now, with the tourists gone."

"Then you could do the same in Italy?"

"I'll telex our post in Rome."

I was feeling desperate again, the blackness rising around me. I was running out of ideas, words, precious words to keep the blackness at bay.

"Well, thank you," I told Helen. "I can't tell you how—how grateful I'll be for anything you find out. God, if only there were something *I* could do. I suppose I could get in touch with Michaelis Kastri. He came back last night, you know. You must have heard."

"What would be the point of that?" Ferrier asked.

"He's one of the Greek friends I mentioned. It's a long shot, but you never know—he might be able to help."

"I'll get busy and send those telexes," Helen said. "Then I'm going for some lunch. Mr. Urquhart, you must need some too."

"No thanks, I'm not hungry."

She gave me a worried look. "At a time like this you have to eat."

It was an unexpectedly human thing to say.

10

I didn't want to be alive. If Nick really was dead, there was no point. I would simply rather go where he was. I pictured a bomb exploding inside my chest, ripping apart my heart, my lungs, my ribcage, my entire skeleton, scattering the smoking pieces to the sky.

On the other hand, here I was, putting one foot in front of the other, walking down Vasillis Sophias Avenue with Helen, and it occurred to me that, as long as I was alive, Nick probably was too. The mathematics of it were simple. And terrifying.

All the constructive activity at the embassy had provided me with a brief respite. Now it was finished, the telexes sent, the phone messages placed. Now the waiting began. And while I waited, terror dodged around the edges of my brain, a sniper seeking an angle.

I tried my best to elude it by focusing on signs of life. A sidestreet called Plutarchou. A funicular disappearing into the slope of Mount Lykabettos, re-emerging at the summit. Specks of human beings up there, moving dots on the steps of the white chapel, beneath a Greek flag. Pedestrians strolling up a sidestreet towards Kolonaki Square. Helen's hair brave and shining, lifting with each step, lighter than the heat-laden air. She was saying we could go to one of the cafes in Kolonaki, but they'd be crowded right now, and noisy, and she was sure I'd prefer someplace quieter. Nodding, I assented numbly, grateful to put myself in her hands.

We ended up walking all the way down to Constitution Square, then turning into a tunnel-like sidestreet shaded by buildings that leaned close together above our heads. The shops were tightly shuttered for midday. Helen suggested an *estiatorion* on a corner, a modest place with a couple of tables on the sidewalk outside, their wooden surfaces scrubbed to the colour of bone.

Sitting down inside the restaurant, I felt my organs shift inside me, another alteration in this rapid succession of states: an exhausted, unreal calm, a hollow resignation. For the moment, I'd done all I could. After lunch I'd keep going. For now it was time to shut down a while. I looked at my watch, subtracting seven hours: it wasn't even nine a.m. back home. Ordinarily, I'd just be getting into my office to begin the workday.

I looked around, forcing myself to become aware of external reality. The restaurant smelled of scalded olive oil and freshly baked bread. Bare fluorescent tubes on the walls gave off a harsh, green, unnecessary glare. Two old-fashioned fans rotated from the ceiling, almost succeeding in cooling the place. The glass doors were wide open to the street. All the patrons were working men, eating with impressive dedication, with singleness of purpose, their elbows anchored on the paper tablecloths that were secured by elastic bands, their mouths working athletically, fingers dismembering great chunks of crusty white bread. I wondered how they could act so normal.

Helen and I declined a visit to the kitchen, offered because I was a foreigner. We both ordered something, and I asked for a *karafaki* of retsina.

The wine arrived first, in a glistening copper pitcher dripping with condensation from the heat. I wasn't sure I wouldn't spill the contents, so I let Helen pour. Slowly, tentatively, I tipped the glass back, let the first freezing sharp-scented mouthful bite the back of my throat. Seldom had anything tasted so good. Yet I felt a strange ambivalence towards the retsina, something precariously balanced between thankfulness and deep mistrust. If ever I was at risk, it was now.

Sure enough, almost immediately the wine began running amuck in my system, shredding my defences, throwing open doors I'd been keeping locked. Tears squeezed out from under my eyelids. I sat very still, trying to outwait the moment. It took a while to pass.

I could feel Helen watching me. She said, "It's terrible for you."

I cleared my throat noisily. "I was letting pessimism get the better of me. Thinking Nick may have been dead for weeks now, for all I know."

"Yes."

"But it's no good thinking like that."

"No."

I tried to look her in the eye, the knowing older man, ready for anything. Even though I certainly was not.

"It's better to keep hoping," she said softly. "After all, people disappear all the time, then turn up as if nothing had happened." She made it sound so eminently reasonable. Not at all like a fantasy.

"That's right. Remember Aegeus? Silly old bugger, he threw himself off the cliff when he saw the black sail on Theseus' ship. Didn't have the patience to find out his son was still alive." This bit of pedantry had a calming effect: a cover for my embarrassment.

The food arrived, along with a pitcher of ice water and a pink plastic basket holding bread, napkins, and tinny cutlery. Helen asked how I'd come to know Michaelis.

She ate as she listened. I couldn't swallow anything, but the talking settled me down, and eventually I ate a few mouthfuls myself while she explained Michaelis' current political standing. As I listened, I was somehow able to keep from drinking too much or too quickly—apparently I'd lost my appetite for alcohol, too.

Helen said Michaelis' stature was still high among those who had known and supported him before the dictatorship. But since then, practically a whole generation had come of age; for the young, Michaelis was a remote figure from the past, who'd enjoyed the freedoms of exile while they suffered under the junta. Now students on the Left were more likely to find their hero in Alexander Panagoulis, the activist who'd tried to blow up one of the Colonels, then spent years in prison before being exiled himself.

"Michaelis was imprisoned too," I pointed out.

"But not as recently. People are fickle. They forget."

Helen had read in the papers that the Hellenic Socialist Liberation Movement had already opened a makeshift headquarters downtown, in preparation for Michaelis' return. The parties of the Left, Right and Centre were jockeying to win leadership of the new order. If there was going to be war with Turkey, Karamanlis and his provisional cabinet would have to wage it, and the other party leaders could hope to pick up the pieces, if any.

I felt faintly encouraged knowing there was a place where I could contact Michaelis. Apparently it wasn't far away. Helen offered to take me there before returning to the embassy.

11

Outside the restaurant, the city was coming alive again. People were returning to work, shopkeepers raising their metal shutters. Numb with dread, I followed Helen into the street.

We walked behind three men ambling along deep in discussion, their hands clasped behind their backs, dexterous fingers flipping long strands of black and amber worry-beads. In a kind of trance, I watched the beads leap rhythmically up and down, up and down, with a life all their own. Ahead of us, a young man and woman emerged from the entrance to an apartment building, their bodies leaning into one another. Oh, to be full of grace like that. I'd done what I could to evade my dread—seeking refuge in Helen, in food and drink, in the hope of seeing Michaelis. Now it was back to the hot city, the implacable pain. If I'd had a God, I'd have asked Him now to give me the strength for what I had to do.

My only plan was to go to Michaelis' headquarters and introduce myself, in the hope somebody had heard of me, or was sufficiently impressed by my connection with Michaelis' years of exile to give me an appointment. I felt sure he wouldn't be there himself yet. He'd be at the suburban villa that had belonged to his father, putting things in order, holding court. Greek political parties were built on loyalty to the leader; the leader's living room was the real party head-quarters. Besides, it would be safer for him there. The army would need a while to get used to his presence.

After a few blocks, we came across a small crowd milling around an intersection. A single policeman stood in the door-way of an office building, confronting three or four dozen excited onlookers and trying, without much success, to keep them away from the entrance. When two army officers joined him, the people knew enough to drop their voices and step aside smartly.

Helen and I moved to the edge of the crowd. She tugged at my arm and said something, but I couldn't hear because some idiot driver was leaning on his horn. A gleaming black limousine was pushing its way through the people, its horn continuing to sound — not in warning, it seemed, but in celebration, a harbinger of good tidings. The car stopped directly opposite the policeman and the two soldiers, who elbowed people aside so the rear doors could open. Then the crowd began applauding: the sound of hailstones hitting a tin roof. Flashbulbs exploded, and out of the limousine, into the sunlight and clamour, rose Michaelis.

In an instant, the world shrank to dimensions I thought I understood.

Michaelis responded soberly to the applause, clearly regarding it as his due. He acknowledged it with a Churchillian salute, cupping his hand as if to grasp the ovation, feel its texture. After a moment, he was about to turn away and enter the building but something made him linger: the applause was being prolonged, growing louder every second, mixed now with cheering — not a mere courtesy after all, but heartfelt.

Michaelis' expression changed then; his sobriety gave way to a grin of sheer pleasure. He nodded several times to different parts of the crowd. Even Helen was clapping. I wasn't — and because of that, Michaelis noticed me. In a gesture of recognition, he gave me a twitch of the famous eyebrows. Then he turned away, before the welcome could lose its vigour, and disappeared inside the building, his companions from the limousine quickly closing around him. Two of the entourage were familiar to me: Costa Marinopoulos, Michaelis' closest political aide throughout all the years in exile, and Stathis the bodyguard, dressed as usual in a shiny black suit that needed a trip to the cleaner's.

I turned to Helen. She was smiling broadly, revelling in the unaccustomed carnival of free speech.

"He saw me," I told her.

"Good!" She pulled some ID out of the purse suspended from her shoulder. "This may get us in."

As the crowd dispersed, we approached the policeman, who had been forsaken by the army officers now that Michaelis was safely inside. Young and overweight and overburdened by a sense of responsibility, the policeman was sweating profusely, relieved that Michaelis' arrival had passed without incident. Now we presented him with a new problem: he glared to warn us off.

Helen pressed her papers on him, informing him we were from the Embassy of Canada, demanding entry before he'd even had time to decipher her ID. With an aggrieved expression he removed his cap. He protested loudly, but his eyes kept returning uneasily to the papers, which Helen now thrust into his hand, challenging him to deny that they were perfectly official and acceptable and invested with a higher authority than his own. It was a matter of who could bully whom.

"Quick," she said to me, "give me a name—somebody in Kastri's party."

"Costa Marinopoulos."

Helen said something about "Kyrios Costa," and the policeman's resolve slipped another notch; he knew he was beaten. Wiping globules of sweat from his upper lip, he replaced his cap to re-establish his dignity, and was still berating us as he stepped aside to let us enter.

The party's offices were on the top floor. We waited in a dim hallway, breathing the cloying smell of damp plaster and old stone, while an antique elevator descended. Michaelis certainly wasn't starting out in the lap of luxury.

Creaking and groaning, the metal cage deposited us at the sixth floor. Stathis the bodyguard was posted there to screen arrivals. He was a stocky peasant with a ruddy face, who spoke mainly with his eyes; now they registered a flicker of surprise.

"*Kalimera*," I told him. "*Ti kanete?*"

"*Poli kala.*"

Stathis permitted himself a small grin. These pleasantries were the only words he and I had ever exchanged, and it seemed to amuse him that now we were speaking them on Greek, not Canadian, soil. His eyes checked Helen out. He didn't bother asking our business, just escorted us down the corridor.

Through an open doorway I caught a glimpse of Costa talking animatedly with another man: Costa who'd been through so much with Michaelis, home at last, his loyalty and tenacity and resourcefulness finally rewarded. He was so absorbed in his conversation that he didn't notice me passing by.

Stathis showed us into an office at the far end of the hall. Michaelis' secretary, Angela, was stationed behind a desk, talking on the telephone, her plump face elaborately made up as always. When she saw me, her mascara'd eyes widened, her mouth made a red O. She motioned to us to come closer, then hung up and thrust a hand towards me in her eager ingenuous way. I grasped it gratefully.

"Mr. Urquhart, what a surprise! What are *you* doing here? He'll be so delighted to see you!" Her eyes sparkled moistly, her hand warm and damp from the receiver.

I introduced Helen, explaining that she was from the embassy, but not explaining why we'd come. I couldn't bring myself to talk about Nick, not there: I was afraid I'd break down in front of everyone. Unaccountably, I was feeling humiliation, an appalling sense of shame and guilt over what I'd allowed to happen to my son. I just told Angela there had been "a family emergency" and I needed Michaelis' advice. I hoped "advice" would sound less burdensome than "help".

"I see. Of course, of course." Angela nodded soberly. "I hope it's nothing *too* serious. Well, we're completely at your service, Mr. Urquhart. Only we're so new yet — absolutely *nothing* is organized and we have only two telephone lines, but we'll do what we can, believe me. What do you need? Interpreter? Typist? I should have a photocopier by tomorrow."

"To tell the truth, Angela, I'm not sure. But if I could just see Michaelis for a few minutes, it would do me an awful lot of good."

"Ah," she said, her brow furrowing. "That might not be so easy. You can imagine what it's like. I'll go find out for you." With surprising grace she rose and unlocked a pair of enormous varnished doors behind her desk, closing them quickly behind her with a loud click. Michaelis was protected by two lines of defence, even if the second was only a simple lock guarded by Angela's desk and ample figure.

Helen said in a low voice, "Better ask him to recommend someone to find Nick. Someone in authority besides the ESA."

She was right, of course: even if I wanted to, I couldn't rely on Drakonakis to mount an adequate search. "What about a private investigator?" I said. "That might be the answer. Do they have them here?"

"Of course." She was surprised at me for underestimating the Greeks' capacity for intrigue.

Angela returned. "He'll see you as soon as he can. Perhaps in fifteen minutes. But only briefly, I'm afraid." She paused to solicit my understanding. "The poor man hasn't slept."

Devoted Angela. She and I both knew my "family emergency" was the last thing Michaelis needed right now. Yet I'd been right to think he wouldn't turn his back on me, not even in these circumstances. He had actually met Nick once — in fact, had made a powerful impression on him during Nick's political phase. I was counting on that to strengthen Michaelis' concern.

The fifteen minutes became half an hour, and the telephone never stopped ringing. Angela shouted at Stathis, in that way she had of pulling rank on him, to bring chairs for us, and Helen and I sat in intimate, inanimate silence while the frantic activity surrounding Michaelis' homecoming swirled around us — a diversion I was deeply grateful for. Finally, Angela's intercom buzzed.

She listened, nodded and said, "He'll see you now."

"I'll wait," Helen called as I passed through the double doors to the inner office.

12

Michaelis sat behind a desk in his shirtsleeves, talking on the telephone. Backlit by dusty sunlight from a single window, stray wisps of grey hair swirled about his temples and framed his great balding head. A burgundy tie hung loose down the front of an unseasonable long-sleeved shirt stained dark at the armpits.

He peered at me above the half-moons of his reading glasses and cupped a hand over the mouthpiece. "It's Theodorakis!" he whispered, his face jubilant. "From Paris! He may join us instead of the Communists!"

Michaelis might be running on little or no sleep, but he was clearly exhilarated to be back, in his natural element at last. I tried to smile in reply. It felt good to be in the same room with him. A long work table adjoining his desk had already begun to resemble his office at the university, obliterated by paper: memos, correspondence, reports and newspapers, always newspapers, in Greek and half-a-dozen other languages.

He and Theodorakis finished their conversation, and Michaelis hoisted himself out of the chair and came around to my side of the desk, his arms outstretched. As we embraced, I stared out the window at the hazy sky, thinking they must have chosen this office because there was no building opposite, no sniper's perch. There was also, I noticed, a side exit from the room, in addition to the door I'd come through.

His bearhug felt good. "Jim, Jim," he was saying, "how are you?"

I didn't answer. We stepped back to look at each other.

"This is quite a day for you," I said. "That welcome down in the street—those people were ecstatic."

"Ah." He grinned. "Not everyone is, needless to say. I paid Karamanlis a courtesy call at noon. Honestly, Jim, he looked like he'd swallowed a worm. Of course he's always dismissed me as George Kastri's brat — irritating, but basically harmless. Now he's shocked to see I've lost my hair like him!"

"You're practically an elder statesman."

"Well, this country makes me young again — not the good grey prof I was in Toronto."

He gestured towards the wooden chairs surrounding the work table. They sat at haphazard angles, as if a meeting had just broken up. "Come, sit." He flopped into one of the chairs, flinging his reading glasses onto a mound of newspapers whose front pages portrayed his arrival. "Of course I have the same old problem here — my image! One of the first things I need to tackle. What I really lack is access to TV."

"That shouldn't be difficult."

Slowly he rubbed his eyes. "You'd be surprised. I have no trouble getting print coverage — even the right-wing press are happy to write about me, it gives them a chance to misquote and slander me at every turn. And the foreign networks are fine — the Swedes want ten minutes later today, same with the BBC and the West Germans. But the Greeks — no sir! The state network is still censoring itself. Insists it needs Karamanlis' permission before it can interview me!"

"You're still a little rich for their blood."

He seized his glasses, leaning towards me. "You know what the problem is? The bastards are too cowardly to seize their freedom while they can. Well, they'll have to swallow me, Jim, all of them, swallow me whole — the network, Karamanlis, the army, the whole damned establishment. *I'll* be the test of the so-called freedom under their new regime."

"So the army's behind this regime too?"

He smiled indulgently. "Can you doubt it? Nothing happens without the consent of the army."

"They've already made such a mess of things."

"Doesn't matter. They're still in control. Ioannides could turn everything upside-down in a minute if he wanted to. He has no objections to being back in power."

71

"I guess I'm naive. I thought Karamanlis was in charge."

"He's useful to them. But they're *essential* to him. That's the difference. He won't exercise real power until he's elected — then the army and the CIA won't dare touch him, because the Americans have called for a democratic Greece."

"So the army's in no hurry to hold elections."

"Exactly. And as long as Karamanlis makes everyone think democracy is on the way, we'll have *stability*." Michaelis pronounced the word with eloquent disgust. "Stability is what everyone's lusting for. If Karamanlis can avoid war with Turkey and make some face-saving deal for Cyprus, he'll be a bloody hero. He'll have carte-blanche. And of course he'll win the elections — if he bothers to hold any."

I wasn't up to discussing Greek politics, yet couldn't help feeling uncomfortable with the drift of Michaelis' thought. "But don't you want to avoid war too?"

He shrugged impatiently. "Not at *all* costs. Have you heard the latest from Cyprus?"

"No."

"Half a dozen Greek civilians killed near Kyrenia. In cold blood. I mean, how much longer do we have to take this? *Nobody* can presume to lead Greece who lets Greeks be murdered!"

Michaelis stared at me from under the thick weave of his eyebrows. I said nothing.

"*Of course* I want peace. I just wonder what we'll have to pay for it. Don't you think Greece has sacrificed enough in the last seven years? The last fifty? A hundred?"

"Michaelis—"

"I'm sorry, Jim. Sorry." He reached forward and squeezed my wrist. "Why the devil am I haranguing *you*? But it's ironic, isn't it? For the sake of saving Greece from war, I'm under tremendous pressure to support Karamanlis in his peace efforts. Meanwhile he's being pressured by the Americans to cave in to Turkish demands. And the whole time the Turks are huffing and puffing and massing troops on our borders, all with Kissinger's blessing."

"Not a happy situation," I murmured.

Michaelis stretched for a Papastratos filter-tip from

the pack on the table—no Kents for him any more—then thought better of it. The last time I'd seen him, he'd given up smoking. Two butts, both smoked half-way down, lay in the black glass ashtray in front of him.

"Anyway, don't worry," he said, with a small grin, "I haven't become a warmonger. Not yet. Now what's this emergency of yours? What brings you all the way here? Angela didn't explain. I was astonished to see you down there in the street."

As calmly and dispassionately as I could, I recounted events to that point. It wasn't easy, so I kept it concise.

Michaelis' face darkened as he listened. Finally he said, "Good heavens above, Jim. You have my deepest—believe me, if it were one of *my* boys—" He shook his head. "Is there any kind of help we can give you?"

"The strange thing," I said, "is I honestly don't believe Nick's dead. There's no solid evidence. No body, no police report—only this prisoner's confession. And for the life of me, I can't believe he's a murderer."

Michaelis thought this over for a moment. "I see. I don't want to discourage you, but—the prisoner has confessed, hasn't he? Why would he admit to such a terrible crime if he hadn't done it?"

"I've thought about that too. I know this sounds irrational—I mean, maybe I'm still in shock and don't know it, maybe I just can't look facts in the face, but I looked very hard at that prisoner today, and I saw a scared, innocent young man, not a psychopath. In some weird way, he reminded me of Nick."

Michaelis looked sharply at me, his brow furrowing. "What sort of condition was he in?"

"Not good. He'd been knocked around a little. Looked like he knew that would only be the beginning. Why?"

For a second Michaelis had seemed concerned about the prisoner's health, but now he shrugged. "Just curious—wondering how the ESA is treating its prisoners. Sounds like nothing has changed. Anyway, go on. Tell me what you'd like us to do."

"Well, the embassy people are trying their best but their

73

scope is limited. They have to depend on the good will of the ESA, their embassy in Rome, etc. I expect I'll have to go there myself to make sure something's being done. And this Major Drakonakis said he'd organize a search for Nick, but there's really nothing in it for him. So I wanted to ask you —can you refer me to anyone else in Athens? Someone you trust, who would take the case over?"

Michaelis nodded slowly, hungrily eyeing the packet of cigarettes. "Someone else would certainly be an improvement over Drakonakis. I've heard of him. Known as 'the Dragon', can you believe it? A Cretan, originally. Great favourite of the NATO boys. He's been on training courses in Brussels and Washington. Used to be with the KYP, the Greek version of the CIA."

Michaelis' intelligence on Drakonakis was remarkably thorough. "Sounds unsavoury," I said.

"To put it mildly. He was in charge of the unit that commandeered the telephone exchange during the Colonels' *putsch*. However. I want to help all I can, Jim. Naturally I'll do everything possible. Problem is, I've been away for six years. Even when I was in my father's cabinet, the army officers I could trust were few and far between. And now— you can imagine how many of *those* are left. If any are, it's because they transferred their loyalties to the Colonels." He sucked the arm of his reading glasses. "Still, I'll ask my people to check around. Maybe Costa can come up with somebody. Lots of civil servants are still closet democrats— although whether they're well disposed to the party, or to me, is another matter."

"What about hiring a private investigator? Someone who'd find Nick if he's paid well enough? I've brought plenty of cash."

"Oh no, Jim," he said reprovingly, "I wouldn't trust any-one like that. You never know who else they're working for."

Michaelis rubbed his chin thoughtfully, then put his reading glasses back on and gazed over top of them. "There *is* one person I can recommend. Someone from my staff."

"That's wonderful. Who is it?"

He shot me a worried look. "You won't feel so glad when

I tell you. Still, in the circumstances she can probably help as much as anyone. Unlike the rest of us, she's been back quite a while now."

A new kind of panic seized me. So that was why he'd worked up to the subject so gradually.

"Good Lord. I see. But why would Maria—would she be willing to?"

* * *

Michaelis pressed a button, telling Angela to send Maria in.

I don't need this, I thought to myself: so help me God, I don't. Yet apparently Michaelis believed it was the only way. There was nothing I could do but trust his judgement.

Preparing for my first sight of Maria in a long time, I could feel my face and neck flushing hot with blood. I imagined reaching for a non-existent drink. It staggered me to realize she'd been in the building, close by, all along.

Maria slipped into the room through the side door, so silently that at first I didn't realize she was there. When Michaelis coughed discreetly I turned around and there she was, standing just inside the entrance, putting the maximum distance between us—her shoulders hunched, hands thrust deep into her pants pockets.

Her long black hair was still parted dead-centre like a schoolgirl's or a peasant's. It gave her face a certain severity: an impression contradicted by the frankness in her eyes, the gleaming fall of her hair as it broke over the shoulders of a black silk shirt unbuttoned, as always, too far down. Her loose linen slacks and leather sandals were acutely familiar. The only change I could detect was a spray of silver in the hair above her forehead.

Staring, neither of us spoke. To my surprise, Maria smiled suddenly, shyly: a betrayal of the hidden sweetness in her. In the circumstances, I couldn't help finding it perverse. When I didn't smile in return, she made a peculiar ducking motion, like someone avoiding a blow.

Michaelis frowned. Maria and I had always been a trial to him, a burden he'd have preferred to do without.

"It's my privilege to bring you two together again," he said. The sarcasm was unlike him. "I wouldn't, needless to say, if I could help it—if I were in any position to help Jim myself—but since I'm not...." He hurried on with a sweep of his hand. "Maria, on the other hand, you are on excellent terms with the powers that be. You have contacts, a deservedly blameless reputation. You'll be able to come and go and make the necessary enquiries about Jim's son. On these grounds, Jim, I'm sure you'll agree Maria is the best person to help you."

I wondered for whose benefit Michaelis had made this little speech—Maria's, obviously, and mine as well, but it had undoubtedly been a speech, not his normal way of speaking at all. He proceeded to explain the reason, flimsy as it was (it seemed flimsier still, coming out of someone else's mouth), why I believed that Nick was still alive despite the prisoner's testimony.

As she listened, Maria's eyes were hooded, hidden from me, her body motionless. She waited silently for Michaelis to finish.

I responded first. "Maria? I don't know what to say. Do you want to do this?"

She turned to me slowly, looked me up and down, and nodded, almost imperceptibly.

"It won't be easy," I said unnecessarily. "For either of us. But I'm grateful. It's kind of you."

Her eyes widened questioningly as she listened, as if I were speaking some alien language. Her gaze laid me bare. I wished she'd look somewhere else.

"I can imagine how upset you must feel," she said finally. "I guess it also upsets you to find me here." Her voice trailed off, strangely small. "But it *is* my home. Anyhow, I'll be glad if I can help. If you want me to."

"I want you to."

We both looked helplessly at Michaelis, appealing to him to speak next.

He seemed satisfied. "Good: that's settled then. Now, I

76

have to do interviews, so I'll let you both get on with it. Good luck, Jim. And when you find Nick, remember to give him my regards."

Was that a thoughtless, cavalier remark? Or was he as confident as he sounded that we'd find Nick alive and well? But clearly he wanted to close the subject, and I was still wondering as I embraced him, wished him good luck and, full of confused misgivings and baffled hope, followed Maria out of his office.

13

I'd always imagined I'd see her again. But not this soon, and hardly this way. I'd pictured a quiet drink, a civilized conversation somewhere on neutral ground: a chance to reassess what had happened between us, to recollect in tranquillity, to make whatever fragmentary peace was possible. And I'd imagined it occurring so far off into the future that we could be philosophical about it, buffered by time. By history.

Now all that theoretical distance had collapsed. The physical Maria was standing beside me on the sidewalk, in the pitiless light, my awareness of her compelled by details I'd tried to forget. The fine, delicate, subtly crooked bridge of her nose. The small brown mole by her left ear, like a beauty spot—mate to one on the inner curve of her hip. Her dark scent, unchanged by time. Her cascading wilderness of hair. Those tapered fingers that lingered thoughtfully on whatever they touched. I couldn't take in the whole of her yet, it was too overwhelming. Just these separate, emblematic fragments.

I was so abstracted I'd almost forgotten about Helen. Having introduced herself brightly to Maria upstairs, she now hovered beside us on the sidewalk, waiting for a signal to leave. In her innocence of the situation, she was happy for me that Maria had "volunteered" to help. Now she could get back to the embassy, assured I was in good hands.

I told Helen goodbye, and how much I appreciated her help. She promised to phone me at the hotel the next day, or as soon as she got any information about Nick.

I watched Helen walk off down the street, disappear around a corner. Still staring at the space she'd vacated, I asked Maria, "Are you ready for this?"

I turned to look at her. The woollen bag hanging from her shoulder was a Cretan antique, embroidered with a geometric pattern in faded reds and blues and earth-tones, natural dyes. I checked my digital watch. A little after six: already into the countdown to the evening's first drink—never mind the difference in time zones.

"Is there a quiet bar where we can talk?"

"You're in Athens, Jim. No such thing as a quiet bar." I kept feeling she was trying to read my brain.

"How about a noisy café?"

"Uh-uh. We can't stay downtown."

"Why not?"

Finally I met her gaze. Somehow I realized I had the same problem she had: I could no longer intuit what she was thinking from her eyes.

"Informers," she said softly. "Every other person could be working for the army. Come on."

I walked along beside her, wondering if the city really was crawling with eavesdroppers and stool-pigeons, or if that was just Maria's penchant for melodrama, given free rein now in her native land. On the other hand, as Michaelis had pointed out, she knew her way around; I didn't. And postponing the first drink wasn't such a bad idea.

We arrived in Constitution Square near American Express. We stood for the next ten minutes waiting for a bus, surrounded by people on their way home. Hot bare forearms pressed in on us. I was suffocatingly aware of the crush of humanity, but Maria didn't seem to care. Neither of us tried to talk.

My sense of unreality was exaggerated by the fantastic heat. I was close to vertigo. Buses came and went, disgorging and admitting passengers, until finally a battered blue bus arrived that was evidently ours: KALAMAKI, it said above a dust-caked windshield. I followed Maria to two unoccupied seats at the rear, near an old ticket-seller smoking a cigarette. When the bus lurched to a sudden stop and our knees accidentally touched, we inched apart automatically.

At first the traffic moved with agonizing slowness. A heavy lassitude surged up in me, exhaustion mixed with despair, sapping my will to question her, even to ask where we were going. Where was Kalamaki? Who was Maria now? I scarcely even cared. What could she possibly matter now that Nick might be dead?

But she did matter. I knew I had to get a grip on myself, a clearer bearing on reality: finding Nick depended on it. It would have been difficult enough seeing Maria at the best of times, but now I needed her, in a way I could never have imagined. Who was she, after all this time? Who were *we*? In some sense, surely, however long-buried, we were still the people who'd met three years ago at the Trojan Horse.

*   *   *

I'd gone to the Trojan Horse, a coffee house on Danforth Road in the Greek district of Toronto, after dinner with Michaelis. The place was packed. Michaelis was being mobbed by friends and admirers, so I sat and drank espresso by myself and listened to the earsplitting bouzouki on the sound system. An attractive woman, boyish-looking despite her long hair, wearing a working-man's checked shirt under a brown suede jacket, leaned across my table, startlingly close to my ear, and asked above the music if she could sit down.

I assumed her reason was that all the other chairs were occupied, but it turned out she wanted to talk. Having seen me arrive with Michaelis, Maria had somehow discovered who I was — she worked as a freelance journalist, and constantly asked questions out of professional habit. Although she looked Greek, she spoke with scarcely any accent and sounded, if anything, slightly English: the result, I learned later, of taking her degree at Cambridge. Without further formalities, she announced there was something important I needed to understand about Michaelis.

What was that, I asked.

Simply, she replied, that the Greek left — the *authentic* left, for which she was apparently in a position to speak —

had nothing but contempt for him.

Oh?

That wasn't just her personal opinion, she assured me calmly. It was the considered view of anyone not taken in by Michaelis' rhetoric and press clippings. He was a careerist, an opportunist blatantly out for himself, shamelessly trading on his father's reputation. He was merely paying lip-service to socialism. He'd adopt some other ideology just as easily if it got him what he wanted.

On Michaelis' behalf, I was offended. Yet also fascinated. This woman seemed too well-spoken, too obviously sophisticated and intelligent, to be dismissed as a crank, a mere ideologue. And her manner suggested she believed sincerely what she was saying.

She went on: it wasn't only the Greeks in exile, with their desperation for a champion, whom Michaelis was using — he'd also been taking advantage of his university post, skimping on his teaching duties. And instead of working on his comparative study of state socialism — the book my firm was expecting to publish — he was writing his autobiography, a flagrant piece of self-promotion, to be published in New York. He'd use it to exploit his imprisonment by the Colonels and pose as the martyr of the Greek resistance. Whereas the truth, as any Greek in Toronto knew, was that he was living the soft life of a pampered professor, thanks to indulgent liberals like me.

Maria delivered her denunciation with disarming charm. Her arrogance took my breath away. For a moment, I wondered if she just enjoyed putting me on, then dismissed the idea. Although her view of Michaelis seemed distorted, even grotesque, I was taken with some exotic mixture of conviction and cynicism in her, expressed as a worldly smile that conveyed as much admiration for Michaelis' alleged chicanery as condemnation. And the implication of myself in the whole business, from some good-looking Greek woman I'd never laid eyes on before, was captivating.

I stoutly defended Michaelis' integrity. Maria and I had quite a set-to above that belligerent music — the first of many such arguments we'd have about him. Somehow, he always represented the essential difference in the ways we looked at the world.

The smoke and noise inside the Trojan Horse were getting to me after a while, so I suggested taking a walk, continuing our discussion outside. Maria agreed without hesitation. It was a warm April evening. I proposed dropping into a local pub for a drink. She countered with the invitation of a drink at her apartment, just around the corner, adding that there was a book of poems she wanted to lend me, which would help me understand something or other about the Greek psyche. We were still disputing over Michaelis (albeit with a dash of burlesque humour), the Greek psyche forgotten, when we fell into her double brass bed.

After that—and in spite of terrible and recurring bouts of regret, remorse, renunciation—I was utterly lost: under her spell, or rather the spell of my obsession with her, for many months. Where I remained until I ripped myself free.

*   *   *

It was therefore ironic that Maria was now working with Michaelis in Athens. The other, sadder irony was that some of her old self-assurance had vanished; she was warier than I'd ever seen her, more closed, self-protective. I knew I was partly responsible for that transformation, and I wasn't happy about it. I mourned for the bright brazen gift of her arrogance.

"I gather you've changed your position on Michaelis," I said at last.

"I've changed my mind about a lot of things. After a year and a half under the junta, Michaelis looks good."

Leaving the worst of the traffic behind, the bus entered a wide boulevard heading out of the city. A median strip, planted with pink and white azalea bushes, divided the roadway. We passed a glass-fronted showroom full of cars for sale, their hoods reflecting fluorescent light that seemed redundant since the sun was still shining. An illuminated sign on the showroom roof said DATSUN, OPEL, NSU, POLSKI FIAT. A competitor's sign up the road announced in English, for the benefit of U.S. servicemen, TAX-FREE AUTO-MOBILES! CITROEN, LANCIA, CHEVROLET.

"I'm getting a sense of déjà-vu," I said.

"What do you mean?"

"Being swept along. Not knowing where the hell I'm going."

"If you want to get off, go ahead," she replied. "I'm not doing this to persecute you."

"I didn't mean *that*."

"What did you mean?"

"I was thinking how completely extraordinary this is— you here beside me."

"We're going to my house. It's easier to talk there."

I knew better than to press her, to ask why we didn't simply talk on the bus. I stared out the window at a small carnival operating from a field beside the road, two ferris wheels and a rollercoaster lit up with pink and blue lights, and nobody, apparently, in attendance. One ferris wheel revolved lazily while the other remained motionless. In the farther distance, an empty stadium awaited the crowds.

I felt a voracious loneliness, a bottomless craving to talk. "So Maria, speak to me. What kind of life do you have now?"

Slouching in the seat, she rested the back of her head against the dirty fabric, then swivelled her gaze slowly towards me: an achingly familiar gesture.

"A good life. I'm glad I came back."

"What do you like about it?"

"Friends. Some of my old chums are still around. And I've made new ones. It's easy, really—people here are quite casual, available. They just drop in on you."

"You regret the years in Toronto?"

She paused a moment, leaving my soul in suspension. "I suppose not. No." Then she added, "It was all inevitable anyway."

"What was?"

"Exile. You."

"Yet you returned here."

83

"Once I accepted there were certain precautions I had to take, it wasn't so bad. Especially when I could see the dictatorship falling. But I couldn't have stayed here through the whole thing, not seven years of it. Living in fear, constantly worried about betrayal.... So everything that happened was ...just life. Don't you think?"

She struggled to smile, but it came out sad. The flatness in her voice made me go cold inside. I moved to safer ground. "How do you support yourself?"

"Translations, a little teaching. There's plenty of work around if you know English. The Greeks want to speak English, the multinationals want to speak Greek. I try to keep them all happy."

"Multinationals?"

"Would you believe I've done work for Esso-Pappas? Not only that, I have a nice little contract with the U.S. Information Agency."

"You're kidding."

"I supply them with a weekly précis of the Greek press."

"Good Lord. What's in it for you? Besides money?"

"Don't ask."

"Next thing you know, you'll be working for the CIA."

Her brow furrowed. "I shouldn't even be telling you this."

"Why not?"

"Your loyalties are unclear, my love. As usual."

That hurt. And I was jolted by her use of our old endearment: a mixed message for certain.

I studied the passing suburban landscape of small shops and apartment blocks. "I'm surprised you live away out here in the sticks."

"Sticks?"

"It's a long way from the action, isn't it?"

"It's inconvenient at times. But it's cheap. I don't have to worry about being bugged, since I don't have a phone. You have no idea what a relief that is. And it's just a few minutes' walk from the sea, so Irini and I can go swimming every day. Of course the water's polluted, but what can you do?"

"How *is* Irini?"

"Blossoming."

"She must be seventeen by now."

"She even has a lover—maybe two. I tell her she has more of a sex life than I do.... Jim, don't look so shocked. You're practically blushing. Still the good Presbyterian?"

I mumbled something about the difficulty of escaping one's roots.

"Exactly."

*   *   *

The bus headed straight for the swelling orange sun as it lowered itself onto the sea, the water dull as gunmetal. Two navy destroyers nestled in the middle distance, and against the glare I couldn't tell if they were Greek or American. A tanker proceeded past them at a stately pace, heading out to sea, blotting the horizon with oily smoke.

We were almost there. As Maria bent to the floor to retrieve her shoulder-bag, her shirt fell open, revealing one of her breasts—she never wore a bra—and the sight of the brown aureole, so familiar once, now so foreign, both excited and angered me. I had to remind myself she wasn't doing it to provoke me. "Oh no," some asinine voice nattered in my inner ear, "the sight isn't intended for you, it's not for your benefit, not yours at all, it's available to anyone, any lecherous citizen of Toronto or Athens or wherever who wants a free look at her body—"

I followed Maria off the bus, alighting near a patch of scummy sand. This, she said, was where she and Irini went swimming when the water wasn't too bad. The circular tanks of an oil refinery reared up a little way down the shore. We walked parallel to a collapsed concrete breakwater, then turned our backs to the sun and waited for the traffic to thin out before crossing the coast road.

Along a sidestreet of walled white villas, branches of pine and eucalyptus grazed the tops of our heads. We passed a house with an enormous red Buick parked in the driveway, an oval USA sticker above Michigan plates. Beside it, a plastic big-wheeled toy lay overturned, abandoned by its young owner. Being favoured by American servicemen and their families, the neighbourhood must have provided Maria with ideal cover.

I set my caution aside: "So why didn't you let me know you were leaving Toronto?"

For answer, I received a gathering, deafening roar. A large commercial aircraft was beginning its laborious climb over our heads, having just taken off from the airport to the south. I saw the Alitalia symbol on the tail.

When the roar finally subsided, she said, "I didn't owe you any explanation. I still don't. I mean, you'd half-destroyed me." After a moment she added, "It's better for Irini here."

"Oh?"

"It's good for her to see me happy. And to stop being a little North American with no values of her own."

"She's pure Greek now?"

"She's happy with what she has. She isn't constantly being tantalized by things beyond her reach."

We turned onto another street, smaller bungalows in tight rows, without elaborate gardens. The luxury of sidewalks had been dispensed with here. Maria pushed open a squawking iron gate, and we entered the small concrete terrace of her home. The house was L-shaped, the plaster washed a sandy rose. Two doors painted orange—the same colour as the wooden shutters—led into each wing. Geraniums grew in clay pots set along the walls, and in the corner several cane-bottomed chairs faced each other like friends in conversation. A small grey cat leaped off one of the chairs, rubbing itself against Maria's leg as she rummaged in her bag for a key.

Inside, she pushed windows and shutters open, and light flooded in, revealing a compact little house. From the front hall, I could see into the sitting room, bathroom, and kitchen simultaneously. Maria disappeared around the corner.

"Irini not home?" I called after her.

"No. Staying overnight with a friend," she called back.

I was sorry to hear that. It would have been easier, in a way, to have Irini there.

In the bathroom a rank swampy smell rose from the

plumbing. After urinating, I washed my hands in the rust-streaked basin and stared at Maria's toiletries arrayed on the glass shelf, a variety of tubes and jars with Greek script and a small bottle of her favourite French perfume, *Le Dix*. I'd caught the familiar fragrance on her earlier. There was a hairbrush, a nail clipper, a box of tampons, a half-empty toothpaste tube rolled up from the bottom. Maria never used makeup or hairspray or deodorants, because she believed it was healthier simply to bathe often, and she always smelled good, like freshly baked bread scented with *Le Dix*.

Her pearl-handled razor sat on the rim of the old-fashioned bathtub. Both pieces of a black nylon bikini hung from the shower nozzle, flimsy straps dangling down. A few dark corkscrew hairs decorated the bottom of the tub — I realized they could be either Maria's or Irini's, now. They moved me, with the power that votive images hold for the faithful. But you're not a believer, I told myself, while a clenched fist in my stomach contradicted me.

14

I entered Maria's kitchen. A pot of cold ratatouille, gelati-
nous but still fragrant with aubergines, sat on the stove.
In Toronto, she'd kept a ratatouille going for days, adding
this and that, then reheating it, distractedly eating the stuff
cold when she was busy with a tight deadline.

I studied a box of Tide on the counter, the familiar
orange packaging. Three women in aprons extolled the product in Greek, photographed as if they were on television,
looking out from three black-and-white screens. Maria's sink,
of course, was piled high with dirty dishes. Unlike me, with
my fussy Scots upbringing, she'd never had much use for
housework. And although her small refrigerator contained
little that was edible, I noticed an uncorked bottle of white
wine and, even more interesting, a large bottle of Votrys
ouzo, nearly full.

"Want a drink?" She'd arrived soundlessly behind me,
having changed her shirt. This one was red silk. Her feet were
bare. Still the linen slacks.

"A little of your ouzo might be nice."

"Water?"

"Is it drinkable?"

"Why? Afraid I'm going to poison you?"

She splashed ouzo into two squat glasses and added a
little water from the tap. Unceremoniously, she handed me
my glass of the cloudy mixture, raising the other to her lips
immediately. We weren't to toast our unsought reunion.

Maria looked sharply at me, as though the taste of ouzo
had brought me into focus. "Remember how you called my
little apartment funky?"

"I do."

"That place meant everything to me after I left Philip. What would you call this place?"

I shrugged. "I suppose it's funky too." I laughed, in spite of myself. "I've told you before—your English has one or two blind spots. Funky was a compliment."

"Not from a bourgeois like you." She smiled—also, I imagined, in spite of herself. In truth, she seemed almost as tense and upset as I was. "Come. Let's talk about Nick."

We went into her sitting room. The cat had taken possession of a deep-blue canvas chair, but Maria pushed the animal onto the floor and offered the chair to me. "The place of honour," she said, settling into an old wooden rocker painted the same deep shade of blue.

Seated, I took the plunge—my first sip of the ouzo, with its mercury colour and oily texture and cloyingly sweet bouquet of aniseed. It lit small fires all the way down my gullet, arriving with nuclear force in my stomach. Immediately I felt droplets of sweat breaking out on my forehead. So, I thought. It begins.

The books lining the shelves were the same ones she had had in Toronto. I sank deeper into the canvas chair, letting my eyes dwell on her. Already I felt at home. In the failing light, her edges actually seemed to be softening, her aura deepening. I should have taken that as a warning then and there.

She set her glass, already empty, on the arm of the rocker. "So how's life with Una?" she asked abruptly, challengingly.

The question puzzled me. "What do you mean?"

"Well, is it everything you hoped for? Are you *happy*?"

Realizing her assumption, I shook my head, nearly laughed.

"You didn't know?"

"What?"

"Una and I aren't together."

"What do you mean?"

"I live by myself. In the same old apartment. Which, as I recall, *you* didn't care much for."

"When—?"

"You should've stuck around to find out."

She stared intently at something that wasn't there, paralysis clamping down on her features. Then grabbed her glass and walked quickly out of the room.

Feeling a certain dumb satisfaction, I polished off my drink. I let go of my fears about Nick for a moment, and thought only of Maria. It was obvious now, here, in retrospect, why I'd been so fixated on her so long, obsessed with her night and day. Her beauty. Her passion. Her mad love for me. So *extreme*. No wonder I'd followed her so far out onto that limb. Impossible to resist what, to me, were her excesses—but to her, just natural feelings.

What had happened between us in Toronto seemed inevitable, as she'd said on the bus: perhaps even worth the cost. Then another jet coming out of nowhere roared overhead, rattling windowframes, ushering back my sense of dread, and I thought of Nick again.

Maria too returned, carrying the big ouzo bottle in one hand and her refilled glass in the other.

"They don't use this flight path often. Just a few times a day."

Without asking, she refilled my glass all too generously, not bothering with water, slopping a little ouzo onto my wrist. Had she slugged some down in the kitchen? I would have.

Sitting down again, sighing, she slowly moistened her lips with her tongue. Her expression became thoughtful now; her understanding of me had undergone a leap, I imagined, a major revision—maybe even a favourable one. She resumed the conversation as if she'd never left the room.

"So why didn't you move back in with her? I thought you two were going to try again."

"We did. I stayed a week."

"And? Changed your mind?"

"Una did. Decided she couldn't stand it. She threw me out."

Maria was silent as she assimilated this. "I'm amazed. You were always so—persuasive, Jim." Perhaps her revised opinion wasn't favourable after all. "And Una seemed so loyal, so attached. I just assumed she'd take you back."

"We were both wrong."

"I'll always remember what you said back then: you and she were going to make 'a new marriage'. You were fascinated with the idea. Like you were inventing some fantastic new consumer product. I felt powerless against it."

"God. Well, she smelled a trap, I guess. Afraid the same kind of thing would happen again."

"Poor Una." This was too much: Maria expressing empathy for her soul-mate Una, when it was far too late to do any of us any good. She asked offhandedly, "So have you any women in your life at all?"

"Oh, the odd date — dinner and lunch and things — you know. No one I care strongly about." Taking a long sip, I managed to resist asking a similar question of her. I wasn't ready to hear about Maria's lovers just then. The unadulterated ouzo was doing its work, numbing the insides of my mouth, my gums, even my cheekbones. "But I have to admit," I murmured, "I'm still not very good at living alone."

"It has its rewards."

"Oh, sometimes. Other times it just seems barren."

She gave a low moan. "*Theos mou*. You and I didn't survive, your marriage didn't survive — why did we do it, Jim?"

"For love, of course."

Her mouth twisted strangely. "I've decided I was only a bit player in your marriage. Strictly supporting cast."

"Don't, Maria —"

"She was always your first love, wasn't she?"

"Chronologically."

"But not your one and only?" Before I could say anything, she answered her own question. "And I was so sure *we* had a great love."

"We did."

"But you never gave it a chance! You didn't have the — the patience. You had to run back to Una. And in her, the essential thing had vanished."

"Meaning?"

"Trust."

Those eyes, those words, homing remorselessly in on my failures through the shadows engulfing the house. I stood and walked to the window and stared past the shutters at the small terrace, eerily luminous in the twilight.

"So what's left?" she said to my back.

I answered without turning around. "Bits and pieces. Parts of families. You and Irini. Nick and I." Then I turned. "That's why we're here, isn't it? To discuss how you'll help find him."

"Remember how you used to set him between us? You're doing that again."

"Jesus, Maria!" She still had her way, so infuriating, of hoarding every memory, every grievance, no matter how painful, and dropping it accusingly at my feet just when I needed it least.

She pressed on: "When Nick was staying at your apartment, you wouldn't allow me to visit. He wasn't allowed to meet me—not even *know* about me."

"Maria, we've been over all this before. I wanted to protect him from—"

"What? Me?"

Taking a step towards her, I spoke with more honesty than I intended to. "No, from me."

"That night you told me to stay away—"

"—for Christ's sake—"

"—I just couldn't bear it any more—"

Ah yes. An evening to remember. Maria on the telephone, unable to take no for an answer. Maria insisting on walking over to my building in the pouring rain, buzzing my apartment and standing outside in the corridor, water dripping off her like a drowning martyr. Maria with hair slicked across her forehead, disputing with me while I refused to let her in, determined to prove I could be as stubborn as she. But Maria pleading and haranguing and refusing to go away, persisting so long that I couldn't stand the scene she was making and finally gave in, telling her she'd have to pretend to be an old friend arriving from out of town who couldn't get a room at the Park Plaza down the street. But she couldn't spend the night in my bed: on that I insisted.

"I had to sleep on your sofa, like a stray cat! Even now I can't believe you did that to me."

"So why did you force me? You were acting so crazy—"

"Was it crazy to love you?"

"Maria, I've had lots and lots of time to think about this. I don't believe it was just *love*. It was a battle of wills—you always pushing, always demanding I give in to what you thought you needed, me pushing back. I had to draw the line somewhere. Otherwise you'd have taken me over completely."

"But why did Nick have to be protected? Surely he wasn't *that* fragile."

I wanted, somehow, to stay calm. To conserve my energy for the real work at hand. I dropped my voice, and in measured, restrained tones, tried to explain. "He was unhappy, confused, his world was falling apart. He wasn't ready to accept another woman in my life. If he'd seen us together, he'd have blamed you for his family breaking up."

This just made her angrier. As if she couldn't stand to hear any more, her upper body lurched forward, propelling the glass from the arm of the rocking chair onto the tile floor where it shattered like a rifle shot:

"*So fucking what?* I *was* to blame! Anyway, my relationship—my love, for God's sake—was with you, not your son!" Less loudly, she added, "So he would've been angry for a while. So what? We could have handled that."

She subsided against the high back of the chair. Carefully, I stepped over the pieces of broken glass and resumed my seat across from her. I was feeling nauseated: didn't know what I was doing there any more. This wrangling over the past was so pointless. Yet somehow I couldn't avoid replying. I pulled my chair closer.

"Maria, I'll tell you exactly how it was for me then. I'd already lost enough—my marriage, my home, most of my friends—I couldn't stand the idea of losing Nick too. He was all I had left." My heart lurched under my breastbone. "He still is."

"You forget you had me," she said dully. "You always saw it as *losing* something instead of gaining something new. When I realized that, I knew we didn't have a chance."

"I didn't have the necessary revolutionary spirit," I admitted. "I didn't answer the call."

By now the house was dark, the deep shadows broken

only by a shaft of streetlight slanting in at a crazy angle across the bookshelves. I hesitated, then, with a hollow sensation of triumph, poured myself a walloping great drink. Poor Maria. Her glass was broken. I could scarcely even taste the stuff as I gagged it down.

"Let me tell you something," I said, reckless now, not giving a damn, "something you never knew because you left before I could tell you. You came back to this wonderful place. A couple of times I drove over to my old house, where I'd spent twelve years or whatever of my life, to pick something up or drop something off or whatever, and I'd find Una dressed up ready to go out somewhere, with somebody, she never said who. And she'd look *sensational*. Glamorous, for Christ's sake. Kind of glowing—full of anticipation."

"So?"

"So I thought, why couldn't she look like that for me, when we were married? I didn't know she could look so wonderful. So vital. And I felt tricked. You know? As though I hadn't really known her all those years."

Maria shrugged. "You and Una were never very free with each other. Maybe she discovered she liked freedom after all."

"It was the same thing when you turned around and went to bed with Philip. You'd been so loving, then you kicked me in the balls."

Slowly and deliberately, as if explaining something to a child, she said, "But don't you see? You'd already done that to *me*. I saw you making up your mind to return to Una, and I thought I'd go crazy. I had no one to turn to but Philip. And it only happened once—with my ex-husband, for God's sake, what could be more banal?—but of course you made me regret it. A thousand times. You acted like I was contaminated, all because of one lapse of judgement. I never thought you'd be so vindictive."

Another wave of nausea, larger and more perilous than the first, crashed over me. Maria stood up. She came dangerously near me, her face suspended whitely in the shaft of light above the red silk, her face like a streetlamp or moon, a ghostly avenging angel, engulfing hair descending, brushing my cheek like wings. What the hell, I thought. Let her win. Only one thing mattered now.

"Michaelis said you'd help," I told the white blur of her face. "Help me find Nick. And all we've done is rake over the past."

"Sometimes you have to rake over the past."

I could feel her breath, her warmth, all over me like liquid. "Don't you realize he may be *dead*?"

"He's not."

"What?"

Peering down on me, improbably huge and pale, she nodded, certain of her triumph.

*   *   *

"Then — he's *well*?" On the answer to this trite question, the balance of my life rested.

"Very well."

"But I still don't understand. Where," I whispered, "is he?"

"In Athens."

"Christ. Where in Athens?"

"I can't tell you." She took a step backwards.

"You don't know?"

"I'm not allowed."

"Allowed? Who's stopping you?"

"Jim —"

"Does Michaelis know?"

"No. Michaelis just knew I'd look after this for him."

Suddenly the flashes of hope and doubt I'd been feeling were full of red anger. I was furious at being toyed with like this, tortured, flayed on the rack. I was like a car without brakes, hurtling towards a precipice. I wanted to stop the car but wasn't sure I could.

"Maria, what are you hiding from me? Why all this cloak-and-dagger stuff? Dragging me all the way out here when you could've told me in Michaelis' office and saved us all this grief...."

"Michaelis' office isn't safe. They wired it before the party ever moved in. We all accept that."

"What's that got to do with it?"

She sighed heatedly, immovably. "It's hard for you to understand, you've never lived in a police state. You learn never to discuss anything important if you're going to be overheard."

"So you've *seen* Nick?" My brain was struggling to catch up with the speeding car, to ask the right question, the one that would trigger the truth, put on the brakes, end the chase.

"Jim, I'm sorry: I can't say any more. I promised. Please be satisfied with this for now."

"Satisfied? Promised who? Who has more right to this information than me?"

"Other people."

"*What* other people?"

"Well—Costa."

"Fuck Costa! You have to tell me—I mean, Nick's my *son*. I need evidence, something to go on, to give the embassy and the police so they can find him for me—"

"No, Jim."

"Has Michaelis seen him?"

"No."

"Costa?"

She laughed weirdly, in some kind of disbelief, right in my face. "No, no, *no!*"

It was her laughter that got to me, shoved the car over the edge. I rose abruptly from the chair and gripped her by both shoulders, her skin hot to my touch through the flimsy silk, and shook her hard—once, twice, three times. Her face went through swiftly ascending progressions of alarm.

"Jim," she cried, "trust me!"

"Maria, don't you see? I can't until you tell me the truth! Just stop being so goddamn secretive!" I'd never meant anything more wholeheartedly in my life. I was practically weeping.

She looked down at my hand gripping her shoulder like a clamp, shook her head, and said simply: "You'll just have to."

Without entirely realizing what I was doing, I slapped

her. My palm was open, and as it struck her mouth it made a short, high-pitched sound, like a twig snapping. The contact felt surprisingly good.

Yet I hadn't wanted to hit her hard — just show her she couldn't treat me like a fool. From the way her hands sprang to her lips, however, then covered her entire face to ward off further blows, I realized I'd misjudged: I'd hurt her.

I placed my hands on her shoulders again, this time to apologize, to console, but Maria tore herself away and went to stand across the room. In a shaking voice, she murmured, "I think you'd better leave now."

I stood there feeling totally bereft, helpless. I didn't want to leave — not until I knew the truth about Nick — but now I had little choice.

"Look, Maria…God, I'm sorry, I didn't know what I was doing…I have to ask you one more time —"

"No."

"Maria, he's my son!"

"Please get out."

I wouldn't get the truth: not tonight, not from her. No sooner than I'd be forgiven.

A moment later I was outside in the hot darkness, bitterly raging inside — furious at myself, maddened to distraction by Maria, longing for things to be different, the way they'd been five minutes or five years ago — yet still moving my legs as briskly as I could past the American servicemen's villas, back to the coast road. I stumbled over invisible breaks in the pavement. My mouth was thick and gummy from the ouzo, my flesh thick with grief and desperation and desire. Thank God there'd been no blood. My legs ached as if I'd run a marathon.

All I knew was I had to get to bed. Had to get some rest before I collapsed. Couldn't take any more. I'd just have to wait for another day, another chance to probe, to enquire diplomatically, to persuade, to cajole, to reason things out. Briefly I considered going into a bright café that beckoned from a street corner, considered getting something more to drink, one more glass of pure self-destruction, then remembered the one thing in the world that could bring me to my senses—that Nick might be all right, that Maria was telling the truth after all, the possibility of actually seeing him alive in this anarchic city or back home or anywhere else in the whole bloody world—and I hailed the first cab that approached along the rim of the ruined sea.

15

I slept that night entombed in dreamless exhaustion. All too soon my nerves jangled to the scream of some inner alarm, and I jolted wide awake — no gentle floating to the surface — to find myself in my room at the Olympic Palace, the morning still unborn, darkness hunched outside my window. Immediately, Maria's insistent claim played back into consciousness: Nick is alive. *Alive.*

I felt a brief, sweet stab of hope. It was succeeded by an awareness of just how hungover-sick I felt, then the irresistible return of doubt: what reason had I to believe her?

Maria had shown me no proof — nothing, beyond her word. What did she really *know*?

I was back into the impasse already, the unspeakable confusion. Not knowing which voice to believe — Maria's or the prisoner's — I sank back into the bed, into a sweat of trembling hope and anxiety, protesting stomach competing with protesting head. Once again I went over Maria's words, intended to reassure me; once again they failed.

Why would she be in any position to know about Nick in the first place? And if she was, what prevented her from telling me the reason, giving me the truth? Truth-telling had always been Maria's way. I'd always believed implicitly in her straightforwardness, no matter how much trouble it had caused: her candour, her honesty.

Whatever Maria's grievances about the past, the wrongs I'd done her — the latest, God help me, being that slap across the mouth — I couldn't believe she'd act out of revenge. Vindictiveness had never been part of her nature. Could she have changed so much? Her bitterness towards me that deep?

I concentrated hard, trying to recall everything my

battered memory cells retained from last night—Maria speaking of Nick, past and present, begging me to trust her; then the cruel paradox of refusing me the very knowledge I needed to be able to trust—and a new speculation seized me, an even worse fear: Maria had never been any good at lying, it just twisted her into knots, imparting a hunted look to her eyes—a look I'd seen in them last night. Oh Jesus. Did she know, then, that Nick *was* dead? And for some unfathomable reason had to lie about it? Throw me off the track?

Pre-dawn traffic sounds filtered through the window, cut off suddenly by the braying of an ambulance, the city calling restlessly in its sleep. I was desperate for the sun to rise, to hurry and rise over me and just maybe over Nick, who might actually be out there somewhere, in some furnished room in Athens—no doubt sleeping more soundly than I.

I'd behaved badly last night. I'd never struck anyone before, outside of a gym or hockey rink, much less a woman —much less Maria. Yet I had to see her again—it might still be possible to get the truth. I couldn't call her, since she had no telephone, and if I took a taxi back to her house, she'd likely slam the door in my face. So it seemed there was nothing, for that moment, to be done. I lay back in the darkness and tried to get calm.

*   *   *

I let my mind wander. I thought about the fact that, since losing both Una and Maria, I'd kept my distance from women, and they from me. Belatedly, I'd taken the counsel of old Duncan, the blunt, tweedy shrink I'd begun seeing in the midst of my turmoil:

"You might consider," Duncan had suggested drily, "going cold turkey on women for a while."

When I asked Duncan why in the world that would do me any good, he replied mildly, trying (but not very hard) to keep reproach out of his voice: "Because it would stop you from kicking them in the cunt."

I knew what he was trying to do: shock me, jar me into acknowledging what I'd done, feeling the pain I'd caused, taking responsibility for it. And he was right. I had no comeback.

For the past year and a half, then, I'd been living womanless. Sometimes I managed it with good grace. Other times, not. It could be difficult for one who'd always believed he loved women, in his own weird way. Perhaps some day I'd emerge from this monkish state and seek out women once again, but not yet. Last night's experience had proved it was still too soon. I was getting an old uncomfortable feeling back, an intimation of myself as dangerous—like one of those creatures in the monster movies Nick and I used to watch.

The movies had remained our one shared ritual after he lost interest in our weekends together at the cottage (Una too busy to join us, reading economics and statistics back in the city), and after he grew bored with professional football down at the stadium beside the lake. Nick had grown too sophisticated to catch fish or cheer the home team any more. Loving him, watching him grow, feeling full of ardent concern and admiring hope, had often seemed a succession of moments like that, when he'd let me know with a withering finality that he'd abandoned the very things I enjoyed most about being a father. I must have done something similar to my father too, I supposed. Yet *that* process, *my* childhood, had seemed endless, whereas Nick's had been over so quickly!

Still, we'd had the movies. At first they'd been science fiction and horror films—later, "art" films from Europe. In one sense or another, they were all monster movies. Our old neighbourhood was home to the Rialto Theatre, a rundown firetrap that had once shown first-run Gable and Harlow films, now reduced to offering double features for two dollars a ticket. There Nick and I saw *Creature from the Black Lagoon, Hound of the Baskervilles, The Invisible Man, Bride of Dracula, Invasion of the Body Snatchers, Curse of the Mummy's Tomb,* and various reincarnations of Godzilla and his atomic breath. More poignant were Chaney's Wolf Man and Karloff as Frankenstein's monster—creatures with souls but without solace. But my favourite was a remake of *The Phantom of the*

Opera, the third version, with Herbert Lom. His obsession with Heather Sears was wonderfully crazy and terrible, and it moved me to helpless tears both times Nick and I saw it together. I often wondered what he'd made of my uncharacteristic display of emotion. He never mentioned it. I presumed that, deep down, his identification with the poor creatures up on the screen was similar to mine.

Eventually we stopped going to the Rialto. Instead Nick became interested in the fantastical beings in the Bergman and Fellini films we saw at upscale cinemas downtown — the chess-playing Death figure in *The Seventh Seal*, the prehistoric sea-creature at the end of *La Dolce Vita*, the enormous mother-whore on the beach in *8½*. Nick had developed adult tastes by then, but here was a thread of continuity with his childhood: the collective psyche of the world's filmmakers remained haunted by monsters.

I always felt those creatures weren't aberrations at all, but the very portraits of our secret selves. All our unspoken, unnameable longings — mine certainly, maybe Nick's too — were exposed to full view up there on the screen. Was that why we both loved the movies so much? And why we never took Una with us?

Yet in truth, she had never seemed interested in going. Even if she'd had the inclination, Una had no room for such frivolities once she began work on her MBA. Something else always had a higher priority: a seminar to prepare for, a paper to write, an oracle to consult at the library. From my own graduate days I knew what pressures she was under, the sudden accesses of anxiety and self-doubt. Nonetheless, one question used to nag me: why, when she already had her MA in English, equipping her to teach high school (as she'd done for several years), or even to lead undergraduate seminars at the university, why did she need an MBA as well? Or to put it another way, why was the woman I loved studying statistics? Economics? *Business*?

"Because they'll take me," she explained more than once, with simple logic and a flash of impatience in her brilliant blue eyes, "where I want to go." And that was senior administration in government. "I don't want to be a nice little harmless schoolmarm all my life."

Let it go, I told myself. Let her do what she wants. But it took time for my heart to catch up with my brain. After all, this was the first issue that had ever seriously divided us. It pressed painfully on some nerve deep inside of me. At that stage of our lives, I wasn't sure I could take the loss of my one and only love, lover, mate, helpmate, to the very same academic rat-race that had once claimed and monopolized me for so long, and that I'd escaped only by travelling to Greece, and by meeting and marrying *her*.

Even so, with time I came around to accepting Una's career aspirations. They were my only rival, as far as I knew, for her affections. All around us, women friends who'd previously seemed happy with their marriages were putting the kids in daycare and going back to work and leaving their husbands. So I was relieved to make peace on the subject. I learned to feel glad of our leisurely, early-morning talks in the car together, when I'd drop Una off at the university on my way to the office — although I usually wouldn't see her again until late in the evening, since she kept long hours at the library doing research.

Even the shared drives ended when Una graduated and won the first civil-service competition she entered, and her ambitions became a permanent reality. She was so eager to make a success of her new job that she started getting up before dawn every morning, doing her stretching exercises, then driving off to work with her bulging attaché case in her new car, in a new direction, without breakfast. A void of unease, of absence, gradually opened up between us, growing wider as time went on. She became absorbed in her work every evening and weekend — an irony, since I'd been trying to cut down on the work I brought home. To fill that void, I looked increasingly to my times with Nick, then becoming fewer and farther between. After that I met Maria.

One evening, when Una had gotten over her compulsion to throw things at me — wine glasses, ashtrays of no particular value, small Inuit *objets d'art* — she tried to approach my infidelity in a light, even bantering tone, as if that would make it easier to cope with:

"Just tell me," she said then. "What does Maria offer, basically, that I don't?"

"Nothing whatsoever, darling, except herself. You're as wonderful as she is. Probably more. It's just that she has time for me."

"Time?" Una repeated with a disbelieving smile. "Time is all you want?"

"She actually seems to *want* to be with me. Says she adores me."

"And I don't?"

"You don't act as if you do."

"That's true: how can I when you're off screwing another woman?"

It was an intolerable situation for both of us. Had our positions been reversed, I would have felt exactly the same as Una. I was behaving impossibly, asking her to accept me at home while I tried to decide what to do with my life. Normally a decisive person, I'd become immobilized by ambivalence; I couldn't find it within me to resolve my conflict. Fierce bouts of remorse and longing for family life were invariably succeeded by an equally powerful desire — somewhere between lust and romantic idealism — for a fresh start with Maria. It was hopelessly unfair for all concerned; yet I couldn't see a clear way ahead. So I started seeing Duncan.

In my sessions with him, I was staggered by the depth of anger that lay directly below the surface of my confusion. It was only to Duncan that I could vent this bitterness towards a wife I thought no longer cared about me — or even Nick — as much as she cared about her work.

"*That's* what gets me," I shouted at him once, "she abandoned us, threw us over! All for a miserable lousy job!"

Nobody should have to live in such a perpetual atmosphere of crisis, I believed, or endure such mutual hostility. It was unhealthy — and for Nick as well. After several more visits to Duncan, I told him that, although it was intensely painful even to think of leaving home, I had no choice — I *had* to go to Maria. At least she wanted me: indeed, was pressing me to leave, to act on my protestations of love. Ending my marriage seemed the only way out.

"If you must, you must," intoned Duncan. "But you're going to find it awfully difficult. You know, Jim, deep down you're a family man. A man of the hearth."

Inwardly I scoffed. Duncan was just a conventionally minded Celt with a sentimental weakness for married life—his own. *His* marriage, I assumed with envy, was just fine, thank you. Besides, it seemed to me that psychiatrists always wanted to adjust you to "reality" instead of seeing you launched on a brand-new course, a higher trajectory.

In the end, Duncan understood me better than I knew. After the initial euphoria of gaining my freedom from Una —my enormous relief at escaping the battlezone our marriage had become—I began to mourn the death of our vast shared emotional history. As marvellous as my new love was, Maria couldn't make good that loss. Couldn't reconcile me with my past. And so I came to be a family man without a family, and without a lover as well.

At the time I failed to realize that I'd begun my mourning even before meeting Maria. My lament for my lost paradise had started while sitting with Nick in the flickering darkness of the old Rialto, watching pathetic scarred Herbert Lom trying to keep beautiful Heather Sears entombed in his foul catacomb beneath the Paris Opera.

16

I n the shower I began to get some strength back. The hot water helped me feel more hopeful that there were still things I could do to find Nick on my own — people I could see, demands I could make. And I still had the resources of the embassy behind me. At the very least, Michaelis owed me an explanation. His role in all this had been outrageous. I'd never imagined I could feel angry towards him. What was the meaning of that manoeuvre in his office yesterday afternoon, tangling me up with Maria again? He knew *something* he wasn't revealing.

I shaved, swallowed some tablets for my throbbing head, and before long was nursing my hangover in the brand-new sunlight streaming through the windows of the hotel dining room. The place was nearly empty, and air-conditioned to a fault. There were exactly as many waiters as customers: three of each. Light bounced crazily off the silver cutlery and pristine tablecloths and starched white jackets of the waiters, who stood about looking bored with nothing to do.

I tried to strike a bargain between the protesting factions in my body — a delicate balancing act between soothing my acidic stomach and supplying my dehydrated nerve endings with liquids and vitamins. I experimented with a few bites from a slice of ripe yellow melon, then proceeded to a bowl of rice pudding sprinkled with cinnamon, all washed down with glassfuls of *gasosa* water from a litre bottle. To finish, I risked a cup of Western coffee — "Nescafé" the Greeks always call it, no matter what the brand — always instant, always served in heavy white cups that are narrower at the top and fatter at the bottom. But the coffee didn't sit well with the other contents of my stomach. The bargain was impossible to strike.

I went outside to the kiosk in front of the hotel and bought an *Athens News*. Although it was barely eight a.m., the heat was already fierce, and I returned to the small air-conditioned lobby to read the paper. More atrocities reported from Cyprus. This time the victims were Turkish. Distraught villagers had led Turkish soldiers to a shallow mass grave in the mountains, where seven corpses had been exhumed. They'd died very recently—two adolescent boys among them. According to the Turkish army, the killers had been Greek peasants from a nearby village, acting in reprisal for the shooting, many years ago, of a relative by a Turk. These acts of revenge were biblical: eruptions of such ancient hatreds that it was hard to realize they were occurring in the present.

Karamanlis was going on television that night. He was expected to present the nation—and of course the Turks and Americans—with his conditions for settling the crisis. Some of his ministers were quoted as saying that, with Greek honour at stake, war was the only alternative. I recognized one of the names, a prominent former supporter of the Colonels. The paper also quoted pro-war sentiments coming from the right-wing press. Things were heating up again. On the Greek side, it was sheer lunacy—their forces didn't have half the men or firepower of the Turks.

I began to feel a sense of discomfort that had nothing to do with my hangover. I was sitting in the eye of a storm. No one was in control any more: not Karamanlis, not the army, not the State Department, not even the CIA. That was the monstrous irony. Although Greece was rid of the dictatorship, a vacuum had opened up which could suck anything and anyone into it. All the semblances of normality around me—meals being served, newspapers published, beds made, bills presented and paid—were simply illusions perpetrated by people who didn't know what else to do while waiting for chaos to engulf them. If only I could count on Michaelis to exercise a sane and moderating influence! But now I couldn't even be sure of him.

I wondered what would happen to Helen Diamantides if war broke out. How bad did things have to get before she was evacuated home to Canada? There would be no such protection for Maria. And certainly none for Nick, if I didn't move fast enough to find him—assuming he was anywhere to be found—and get us both out of there.

Maria had admitted Costa was the key. I decided to see him first. It would be easier than getting in to see Michaelis again, and just as useful. Whatever Michaelis knew, Costa knew a split-second later, and vice versa. That was one thing I could count on.

17

My reception at party headquarters was very different from the day before. No policeman guarded the entrance this time, no soldiers had been dispatched to ensure Michaelis' safety. Evidently the passing of one day without incident was enough to allay official concern. Like any brush salesman or assassin, I walked right inside and took the elevator to the top floor.

Stathis, stationed at his post, didn't act particularly friendly, but I didn't think twice about that—he was normally on the side of surly. When I approached Angela at her desk, however, I began to feel distinctly unwelcome. Her smile had vanished. She pursed her lips, mouthing "Good morning" without addressing me by name.

I asked her if Michaelis would be coming in. Before I could explain, Angela pressed a manicured finger to her lips for silence.

"Angela," I said as softly as I could, "I want Michaelis to know—"

She squeezed my wrist to quiet me. Her touch was oddly reassuring. Without speaking, she handed me a folded piece of paper.

It was a hurriedly sketched map of streets in downtown Athens, their names scrawled in a hand I didn't recognize. It showed the way to a square in the Plaka, located between the cathedral and the Acropolis.

At the bottom, I read: "Please come here (alone) as close as possible to 10 a.m. Costa M."

"Can you find it?" she whispered.

I nodded.

"It's not far." She worked up an encouraging smile.

Down on the sidewalk, I hesitated, wondering if I were being drawn into some kind of blind alley or trap. But I had no choice in the matter; I had to play Costa's game. I studied the map to get my bearings, then started up a narrow side-street. Two motorbikes roared past as if on a freeway. I emerged onto Ermou Street. The colonnaded shops reminded me of Paris or Madrid, fashionable women cruising the expensive dresses and shoes and jewellery and designer luggage, window-shopping in twos and threes like schools of colourful predatory fish. They could afford to take the morning off while their housekeepers queued up for food back in the suburbs.

With three-quarters of an hour before meeting Costa, I slowed my pace. I lingered to observe the graceful aquiline noses, dusky olive flesh, almond-shaped eyes framed in charcoal, filmy dresses uncrushed by the heat. Those hairstyles had required time and money. Even the university students, in their simple white shirts and blue jeans, looked elegant. One of them reminded me of a younger Maria.

Catching the reflection of a hungry-looking man in a shop window, I left the women behind. I went left for a block, crossed Mitropoleos and entered the street encircling the cathedral.

I tried to locate the spot where Una and Nick and I had stood in that sea of humanity during George Kastri's funeral, six years earlier. The mob had been so vast that day, so undeniable, it could have smashed the dictatorship with a single blow. All it would have taken was a concerted march on the palace, a long vigil, a mass refusal to leave, and eventually the demonstrators would have triumphed over the Colonels, would have ceased to be mourners for their country and become its liberators. How could the regime have jailed a quarter of Athens?

But the mob, as huge and passionate as it was, had been a headless monster. It had no mind of its own, no leader to rally it to concrete action. After rampaging for a couple of hours through the streets between the cathedral and the cemetery, paralysing the city and shouting itself hoarse, the mob went home for dinner. The opportunity was lost. It might as well never have happened. The Greeks continued living under dictatorship for another half-dozen years: a depressing thought.

Of course the people had felt impotent against the army. It had been the usual dilemma: nobody, Greek or otherwise, had been prepared to fire a shot to defend democracy in its birthplace. Not I, certainly. There had been no Byron that day.

The only real hero had been the fanatical Panagoulis, who'd tried to blow up one of the Colonels driving past in his armoured Lincoln. Due to some technical problem, the dynamite had failed to detonate, and Panagoulis had been captured and tortured for his pains. But that was what it took: a fanatic in the cause of freedom, someone crazy enough to kill for democracy—crazy enough, too, to oppose not only the fascists, but that other democracy, the United States, which had kept the fascists in power.

The students at the Athens Polytechnic had been crazy that way. A year ago, they'd observed a memorial service for Michaelis' father by occupying their classrooms and tearing down the Colonels' beloved posters and insignia. They'd barricaded themselves inside the Polytechnic walls, broadcasting appeals from a clandestine radio station for a worker-student alliance to overthrow the regime. Nobody knew exactly how many had died after Ioannides sent in the tanks. The regime conceded a few, then twenty-five—not counting the wounded. Eventually, an actual thirty-four corpses were accounted for. Michaelis had once told me it could have been several times that many—Athens was full of stories about young people who had vanished, disappearances that couldn't be explained any other way. Now he was pressing Karamanlis to conduct a full investigation into the massacre. Even at that, it might no longer be possible to document the truth.

I left the cathedral to the ghosts of memory, of vanished possibility, and entered the puzzle of congested lanes rising through the Plaka to Costa's square. Sticking to his map, I went up Adrianou Street, passed a silversmith's, a shop selling ikons and other religious paraphernalia, a window arrayed with dried figs and almonds. A butcher in a blood-stained apron was doing good business, his shop wide open to the street. Red sides of beef and headless pigs hung from hooks perilously close to a lounging mongrel and a hole-in-the-wall autobody shop. Above the stores, people lived in tiny flats behind rickety wooden balconies sprouting grapevines and TV antennas. A television commercial blared frantically into the street, while two women held a conversation from windows facing each other above my head.

After confirming that a street sign in Greek said the same thing as the Roman letters on my map, I realized I was standing in a very familiar spot. It seemed I couldn't avoid the cul-de-sac of memory. An overhead fan blew the rich sweet odours of a bakery into the street, the same bakery where Una, Nick, and I had once repaired daily for coffee and honeyed pastries, *kourybyedes* smothered in powdered sugar, sheep's-milk yogurt sprinkled with cinnamon. All the familiar delicacies were still being displayed in long shallow pans in the window. And of course: just down the street was our old square. It was the map's destination, the meeting place decreed by Costa.

The little square was a rare leafy oasis in that car-choked city. Quiet at the moment, by evening it would be seething with life. How often the three of us—a family!—had eaten dinner at one of those tables among the trees, under the bare lightbulbs dangling from the branches, served by waiters dashing back and forth through the traffic circulating around the perimeter—swift, heroic, devil-may-care waiters, princes of the square, bearing heavily laden trays poised miraculously on their fingertips. This morning fewer waiters were in evidence, moving at a more stately pace, as they carried coffee to clutches of men sitting over newspapers and card games.

I went among the trees and sat down at an empty table removed from the other patrons. No sign of Costa yet—I was still early. Just as well. I could rest for a moment, digest the experience of finding myself in a place where my family had once been—I could have sworn—happy.

Una and I had discovered the square during our first time in Greece, shortly after we'd met. The place had an oddly archaic name—something like "Square of the Singing Courtesans". Physically it hadn't changed much. Three cafés still co-existed around its edges, there was the same suspicious odour when a breeze blew from the direction of the underground lavatory, the same cinema showing godawful Greek comedies, descendants of the same famished cats prowling for scraps under the tables.

Una's hair had been long then, pulled back into a ponytail. Her light blue eyes had been opalescent in the blazing sun, which made freckles emerge on her nose and turned her cheeks pink, then brown, above her delighted white smile. She smiled easily, laughed a lot, in those days. Outwardly she remained the proper sorority girl—cotton print dresses, plain blouses with long full skirts that swirled around her long legs, never slacks, because she didn't want to offend conservative Greek sensibilities. At night she'd wear a pale blue cashmere sweater that made her look even younger and more innocent, carrying her things in a leather shoulder-bag bought in a shop a few blocks from where I was now sitting.

But in a real sense, the *raison d'être* for both of us then was eros. Beneath Una's girlish persona, I discovered anything but innocence. With a tremendous visceral hunger, an astonished awareness of power, we dedicated ourselves to discovering each other's bodies, discarding every vestige of our remaining virginities, technically lost earlier. In the translucent Greek air and ravaging heat, we felt free to satisfy our appetites for the sight and touch and taste of flesh. It was somehow more permissible, more natural, there. In my naïvety I was startled, then excited, to discover she could be as enterprising in bed as I. With surprising rapidity her hair turned a lighter shade of red, shining in the sun like a healthy animal's pelt. Her skin peeled, but she didn't care. She was the happiest and most relaxed I've ever seen her.

In Athens, then on Crete and other islands, we wandered

hand in hand in a kind of trance, immensely grateful just to be exploring Greece, the world, through each other's eyes and bodies. Even at the time I realized how lucky I was: this opportunity, this richness, this reincarnation of Baudelaire's *luxe, calme et volupté*, might never come again. I had a sense this would be our moment of grace, before we returned to the restrictions of home, the trappings of social responsibility. After evenings in the Plaka, in this very same square, we'd return to our ascetic shuttered room in the Hotel Kimon on Apollonos Street to make endless love. And once again I saw, like some hungover guardian angel watching over the smashed palace of my marriage, the slim young sunburnt bodies urgently tangled on damp sheets....

*   *   *

I was so absorbed that at first I didn't notice Costa standing beside me. I stared blankly up at him: he was waiting to be invited to sit. In his white suit and sky-blue shirt and polished shoes, he cut an elegant, dandyish figure beneath the mop of dark brown curls. He was carrying a burgundy leather briefcase—his charming smile, like Angela's, denied to me today. His eyes were subdued, grave. He'd reached middle age overnight.

I stood to shake his bony hand. Setting the briefcase gently on the ground, Costa removed his suit jacket and draped it carefully over the back of his chair. He sat down, pulled his tie loose, and unbuttoned his collar, each gesture orderly, well rehearsed.

"How do you like your coffee," he said.

"A *metrio* is fine." I visualized a nice little shot of Metaxa brandy with it, just the thing for my hangover and for chatting with Costa Marinopoulos, and dismissed the idea only with difficulty.

Costa clapped his hands once, causing a waiter to materialize from one of the cafés, and brusquely ordered two *metrios*. With that business, essential to any Greek transaction, out of the way, he turned to face me. Tiny droplets of sweat stood out on his tanned upper lip.

I didn't know Costa well. I'd run into him a couple of times on my visits to Michaelis at the university, when party business couldn't wait and Costa's arrival had interrupted us. He'd always seemed a sharp-minded and complex fellow —I used to think it would be interesting to get to know him some day, but there had never been time. Now I wished there had been.

"What do you think of the Nixon rumour?" he asked casually. His nonchalance seemed affected.

"What rumour?"

"That he's going to resign. Before he can be impeached."

"I wouldn't have thought American politics were on your mind just now."

"You're right, actually. I'll tell you another rumour: Karamanlis may remobilize the reserves. The army thinks this ceasefire can't last much longer. They don't want to be caught flat-footed."

"Wouldn't that be dangerous?"

Costa shrugged. "What isn't?"

"What would Michaelis do if he were Karamanlis?"

"Same thing probably. The problem, as usual, is keeping the army appeased. If you don't rattle the sabre, the officers accuse you of being soft on the Turks—dishonouring Greece and all that."

"So the leader has to walk a fine line."

"Right. Somewhere between sounding tough and actually doing something."

"What I can't understand," I said conversationally, "is why you people endanger your whole country for the sake of Cyprus."

Costa opened his hands and spread them wide. "Very simple. Cyprus *is* Greek—historically, culturally, spiritually. You should know that, Mr. Urquhart. Only not, at the moment, politically."

"So you and Karamanlis and the army all think alike on that."

Costa rediscovered his winning smile, presenting it to me

115

like a reward. "Greeks have to be united about *something*."

I shifted in my chair. "Costa, I'm flattered you'd take the time to come and talk to me. You're a busy man right now."

"You know, I really should be in Pangrati, making arrangements for Sunday's rally."

"So you know how badly I want to find Nick. Maria must have told you. Or Michaelis."

His voice dropped. "That fellow you went to see in the ESA's prison yesterday—his name was Yannis Antonopoulos, by the way—"

"Was?"

"He's dead."

It was as if he'd punched me in the stomach. The wind went right out of me, my breath coming in short, rapid gasps. That boy in the cell shouldn't have meant a thing to me. Yet suddenly I found myself shaking inside—he'd been my only tangible link to Nick.

"Young men are supposed to be able to take a lot of punishment," Costa continued. "Drakonakis and his goons didn't know Yannis had a heart condition. He didn't tell them."

"But you did know." I shook my head. "Oh no, Costa. This is terrible." Remembering how I'd grabbed Yannis' shirt collar, making him throw himself to the floor of his cell, I felt a painful stab of guilt, of responsibility for his death. Yet hadn't he brought me to Athens in the first place? By stealing and forging Nick's passport, even claiming he'd killed Nick, putting me through a torture that still hadn't ended?

"So you see, Mr. Urquhart. If it *had* been your son in the prison cell, he might be dead now. Actually dead."

"You're telling me he isn't?"

"That's right. But first you've got to understand what Major Drakonakis and his kind are all about. They're about false accusations. They're about torture, extorted 'confessions', murder. And they don't care who it is—Greek or foreigner. Not as long as their ends are served."

I forced myself to be patient. "It's incredible they're still doing these things."

"The only way to stop the bastards is put them on trial

for their crimes. That's what Michaelis is demanding. But we don't think Karamanlis has the guts."

There was a silence.

Finally I said, "All right, Costa. Please explain how this is connected to Nick. And why you think he's still alive."

"I've come here to prevent you from making things worse."

"I beg your pardon?"

Costa leaned back casually, as if we were having a pleasant chat between old friends, but lowered his voice still further so I had to strain to catch his words.

"Did Maria ever talk to you about Alexander Panagoulis?"

"I suppose. And I've read about him. In fact I was thinking about him on the way here. Why?"

"Well, as you probably know, the ESA released him last year. Of course he had to leave the country. He knew the ESA would find it much easier to kill him as a free man than as their prisoner. He didn't go far, just to Italy. There he resumed his little plots against the junta, absurd adventures really, without a hope of success. Yet Major Drakonakis and his superiors still believe Panagoulis to be a dangerous enemy. And they believe Yannis Antonopoulos was one of his followers — his accomplice in another plot against the dictators, just before they abdicated."

"Why would the ESA care about that now?"

"They're looking for a way to protect themselves from prosecution. If they can manufacture evidence of plots implicating the left, Karamanlis will be interested. He'll conclude the ESA is still essential to anyone who rules Greece, even a so-called democrat. And he'll leave them alone." Costa hesitated, then added, "They also think they can implicate Michaelis in this. Then Karamanlis will *really* have something to thank them for."

"*Was* there a plot?"

Costa was silent while the waiter served our demitasses of coffee and two tall glasses of ice water. I gulped down half of my water immediately.

"That's hardly the point, is it?" Costa murmured over the rim of his little cup.

"What did you mean, I could make things worse?"

"You've noticed you're being followed?"

"Heavens no. What makes you say that?"

"I have information they're watching you."

I almost laughed out loud. "Me?"

"The ESA have practically unlimited manpower. However unwittingly, you're connected to their Panagoulis scheme. So they've put a tail on you, just in case it produces something. And what do you know? Both yesterday and today, you go to see Michaelis Kastri. What could be better? You're playing right into their hands."

"Come on, Costa. How am I connected to Panagoulis? I couldn't possibly be used against Michaelis."

"Forgive me, but the ESA don't confine themselves to the truth. Now that they've killed a prisoner, they have to invent a bigger scandal to cover it up. You come along, a foreign friend of Michaelis — you visit Yannis Antonopoulos in prison — you then come directly to party headquarters. How easy for them to twist those facts and use them against us."

"That's nonsense. My only motive for coming here is to find my son. As it turns out, he may be dead — Maria and you claim he isn't, yet refuse to tell me where he is. So who's lying? Who's plotting?"

"All right, I'm coming to that. Please keep your voice down. I understand your position. Try to understand ours. I have to *insist* you stop coming to our offices: stop trying to see Michaelis. I know that's hard, Mr. Urquhart, but this isn't Toronto. The future of Greece is at stake now. This nation is going through a rebirth, it could be on the verge of a true renaissance, to which Michaelis and our party are absolutely essential. That's far too important to be jeopardized by your personal problems."

I had to work to keep my voice under control. "Listen, if you'll just stop playing games for a minute and tell me the truth about my son, I'll cheerfully leave you all to your bloody renaissance."

He looked wearily at me. "I'm trying to. Your son is alive and well, Mr. Urquhart. Here. In Athens. Just as Maria said."

"How the hell do you *know*?"

He reached down to unlock the briefcase. Setting it on his knees beneath the table, he reached inside with one hand, and I heard a metallic click, then—eerie sensation—a faint, electronically distorted voice began speaking in competition with surface hiss on the tape, doing a bad imitation of Nick. The impersonation was so poor that for a second I didn't realize who it was supposed to be:

"Hi Dad. It's me. I'm taping this in a hurry, so I can't say much. Sorry to have put you through all this. I guess it couldn't be helped. At least you like Greece, maybe you won't mind coming here too much. I can't go into all the reasons I'm here yet not here, so to speak—that will have to wait until another day. Please don't worry, though, I'm fine, among friends, nothing to get upset about. One of these days I'll explain the big mystery. Maybe we'll get together in Toronto at one of your favourite restaurants for a nice expensive dinner—your expense of course—and laugh about this. For now, I just want you to go back home without worrying. Okay? I'll write. I'll get home soon as I can, maybe try to get back into school. In the meantime—give Mum my love. If you ever see her. This is Nick signing off. Bye."

Costa pressed a button on the machine. He hadn't taken his eyes off me for a second. To my surprise, I felt devastated that the tape had stopped. As false as the voice had sounded, I wanted to hear more—wanted to be convinced, to believe. My reason was overwhelmed by a turmoil of anxiety and frustration.

"So basically," Costa murmured, "there's nothing for you to worry about."

I returned his gaze, my anger mounting, getting the better of hope—the same anger I'd felt last night when Maria was trying to manipulate my trust.

"Don't be absurd. That didn't even *sound* like Nick. You're going to have to dig up a better actor than that."

"Actor?" His eyes narrowed. "Jesus, you're impossible. Here we practically serve up your son on a platter and you still won't trust us. You ought to be grateful. Do you realize the trouble we went to, to make this tape?"

I laughed bitterly, shaking my head. "You and Maria

must take me for an idiot."

"Bullshit. You heard your son. He wants you to go back home. What more do you want?"

"I want to know exactly what *you* have to do with him —you and Maria. And Michaelis, for that matter. I want to know why you're all lying to me. What's in it for you?" I interrogated Costa's shrewd, handsome face, trying to divine what he was concealing.

Slowly mopping his forehead with a clean white handkerchief, he decided to take a different tack. "Let me ask you something. What would satisfy you that Nick is safe— that he no longer needs your help? How about my guarantee, my solemn *promise*, that he'll be assisted—physically and financially—to leave Greece safely? So he can return home whenever he wishes?"

This was preposterously vague. Yet Costa's apparent sincerity, his earnestness of tone, almost persuaded me to set my doubts aside.

"My God, I'd need far more assurance than that. More details. Especially after this number with the tape. But—well, in principle—of course. Only there'd still be the problem of his stolen passport. I've been to my embassy and they—"

Costa waved his hand impatiently. "Passports are unimportant. They can be fixed."

"Just a minute. I don't want Nick exposed to any more trouble with the authorities."

"It's far less risky than ending up in one of Drakonakis' cells."

"Why should that happen?"

"The ESA are looking for him, aren't they?"

"Yes—because I asked them to! And if they can find him, I'll be delighted. He's just a missing person, for Christ's sake, not an enemy of the state. He's done nothing illegal."

Costa gave a mirthless laugh that made me very uncomfortable. "You don't have to commit *real* crimes to be imprisoned in Greece." His expression turned sour. "You don't give a shit what happens to Michaelis, do you? Or to Greece? Not as long as you find your precious son. Well, I'm warning you, Mr. Urquhart: don't try to work through the ESA. Because if you do, Nick will be the first to get hurt. And you may never, ever, see him again. Now I really must go."

Glimpsing the tape recorder as he returned it to his briefcase, I had a feeling there was something familiar about it. But before I could detain him any further, Costa stood up, turned his back on me, and stalked off across the square under the trees, his white jacket draped over one arm, leaving me with the half-finished coffees and the watchful, starving cats.

I stared after him in numb confusion. I seemed to be alienating my allies one by one. Losing the friends who should be helping me, helping Nick.

I felt an intimation of despair. Maybe Costa was right: maybe I was the biggest threat to Nick after all.

18

Paralysed, I stayed sitting in the square, replaying the tape in my head. I had to decide whether my first assumption had been correct: that this had been, in fact, just another botched attempt to impersonate Nick.

But each time I summoned back the recorded voice, the less sure I felt — and the more it began resembling Nick's voice after all. Was I merely willing it to be genuine? Had I forgotten what he really sounded like?

In a way, the voice *had* been his. The words themselves had been entirely plausible — the references to Una, to my fondness for eating in good restaurants back home, his time-honoured manner of addressing me with a mixture of reassurance (Don't worry, Dad, I know what I'm doing) and defensiveness (So keep your distance). But the timbre, the delivery, had been off-key somehow, not Nick's style or intonation. Even the accent had seemed wrong: the work of someone whose first language wasn't English.

It was terrible not to be able to trust my own instincts. Or the motives of my friends. I was desperate to hear the tape again — yet I had to admit, it had already changed something for me: tilted the balance of doubt in the direction of Nick's survival.

Throwing drachmas on the table to cover the bill, I pushed myself out of the chair and followed Costa. As I hurried along in the direction he'd taken, I thought how the tape must have been made sometime during the night, or else early this morning. So if it *had* been Nick, he couldn't be far away. But then, why wouldn't he want to see me in person? And what reason could he have for wanting me to leave without seeing *him*? Those were questions that disturbed me more, in their way, than anything else.

I also remembered where I'd seen the tape recorder before: Maria had used one just like it when she did interviews for her freelance assignments. Had she made this tape also, giving it and her machine to Costa to play back to me? That would mean — even stranger — that Maria had been with Nick.

I rushed down Adrianou Street, well past the point that Costa would have reached by then, but saw no sign of him. Doubling back, glancing into the shops and small cafés, I realized he must have taken a different route, perhaps a shortcut back to party headquarters — or perhaps to some other destination entirely. In that maze of Plaka streets, there were a dozen different turnings he might have taken; it was hopeless to try to guess which one.

I wandered aimlessly for a while, temporarily lost in the back streets, among the hodgepodge of tattered old houses and garish *tavernas* not yet open for business. I considered going directly to Michaelis' office and demanding to see him. Or else simply waiting there for Costa to return. Then Costa's prohibition came back to me, his warning about "not making things worse", and I hesitated. Should I just back off? Trust Costa and Maria and Michaelis after all, and for that matter Nick — or whoever it had been on the tape — and go back home?

But I couldn't. It would have been irresponsible, even foolish. I had to have my answers.

Turning a corner, I came face to face with the steep, buttressed foundations of the Acropolis perched on its pile of limestone. I stared at the massive ancient bulk of it, gawking like a regular tourist, then slowly turned around and looked about me in all directions — just in case Costa had been right, and someone was following me.

No watchers in sight. I was sure of it. The narrow streets were still quiet; anyone who was without some clearly legitimate purpose would look conspicuous there. Apart from a bronzed Teutonic couple in their sixties hiking briskly up to the Acropolis, the people I could see all appeared to be local folk going about their business. Could Costa's spy be that labourer chatting familiarly with a housewife as she rinsed down her stone steps? Unlikely. That young teenager pushing his moped up the street? The black-cassocked, grey-bearded priest buying tomatoes on the sidewalk? Although I had no experience of being followed — no personal knowledge of what know-it-all novelists call the prickling sensation at the back of the neck when you're being watched — I suspected Costa had just been trying to scare me off. He was doing too good a job.

And for that matter, what had he meant by claiming he could "guarantee" Nick's safety? Just how would he accomplish it? If only I hadn't let that one slip by! I should have pressed him, demanded he explain what the hell he was talking about.

I felt discouraged now, oppressed by the heat. And yet, as I descended the back streets parallel to the walls of the Acropolis, the solidity of those giant blocks of stone was reassuring. If the goddess still inhabited the Parthenon, maybe she was looking out for me, even if the ESA wasn't.

* * *

By the time I reached my hotel it was nearly noon. While the odds that Nick was alive and well seemed to have improved, I also felt, paradoxically, as if I'd lost him. Or rather, that he wanted to lose me. I needed someone to talk to — someone disinterested, objective, who could help put things in perspective. The only person I could think of was Helen Diamantides. My room had a telephone, so I might as well start using it, saving myself some time and energy instead of walking all over town.

Then I remembered all the talk about telephones being tapped. I was starting to think like a Greek. Although I didn't want to get paranoid, better safe than sorry: I used one of the phones in the hotel lobby to dial the embassy.

When Helen came on the line, she sounded tense, distracted. I asked if she or Ferrier had heard anything more from Major Drakonakis.

"I spoke to him this morning."

"What did he say?"

"Nothing new, I'm afraid. The prisoner is sticking to his story."

"Has he come out with any more details? How he did it? Or where?"

"Apparently not. He isn't talking at all, Drakonakis says."

I exhaled sharply. "Of course not."

"I beg your pardon?"

I hesitated before telling her. But there had to be someone I could trust.

"Helen, I have good reason to believe that prisoner is dead."

"Oh my God. Why?"

"I'll explain later. So if Yannis did kill Nick, he'll never tell us any more about it. Whatever he knew died with him."

"Listen, I don't think we should talk this way. Can you come over here?"

"Right away?"

"I have two appointments in the next hour. How about one o'clock?"

"I'll be there."

*　　*　　*

I hung up and took the elevator upstairs. Stepping out at the fifth floor, I had a premonition, even before unlocking the door to my room, that it wasn't empty. I inserted the key and entered slowly, watchfully.

But it wasn't the ESA waiting for me. Sitting by the window in my armchair, reading a newspaper behind a pair of dark glasses, was Maria.

Somehow I wasn't surprised. Perhaps a hint of *Le Dix* had been lingering in the corridor. I felt a surge of elation: I was going to get my second chance with her after all. Taking in the casual way she inhabited her dark blue silk shirt and black slacks, I felt a physical excitement mounting in my limbs.

Maria didn't speak. She moved quickly out of the chair and steered me by the elbow back into the corridor, closing the door softly behind us.

With a certain admiration I asked, "How the hell did you get in there?"

"I told the desk clerk I was your wife and I'd forgotten my key. He didn't dare contradict me."

"So why didn't we talk in the room?"

"The ESA may have wired it."

"You're starting to sound like Costa. He thinks they're following me."

"They probably are. The real source of their power isn't guns, it's knowing everybody's business."

She removed the dark glasses. She seemed remarkably calm, unafraid. With relief I saw no sign of damage to her face. Her eyes were just a little bloodshot.

"I want to apologize for last night," I began.

She waved that aside. "Never mind. We haven't much time. Did Costa play you the tape?"

"On your machine. Did you make the tape too?"

She shrugged. "Costa thought if I couldn't convince you, surely Nick would."

"I'm not convinced that *was* Nick."

"Oh, it was Nick all right." She looked closely at me and frowned. "You don't trust anyone any more, do you?"

"I think you owe me an explanation."

"I know, but there isn't time. Wouldn't you rather see Nick in person?"

"You'd do that?"

She sighed. "It means going against Costa—God knows what he'll say when he finds out. But it's pretty obvious you won't be satisfied till you've seen Nick. Besides, I've been thinking about what you said last night. About him being all you have now."

I could scarcely believe this: I wanted her to keep talking, so I remained silent.

"If you agree to be very careful, and follow my instructions

126

to the letter, I can send him to you."

"I agree."

"Come on, then. This isn't a good place to hang around. I'll explain in the elevator."

First we rode up to the top floor to give us a little more time, then down to the lobby. Meanwhile Maria gave me her terms: she still couldn't tell me where Nick was staying, but she'd bring us together in a safe meeting place, as long as I told nobody where I was going.

I began to believe her. "You're serious about this."

"Of course I am. But this time," she said acidly, "no more questions. All right? And don't let *anybody* know—not even your nice little embassy friend. Costa would kill me. Besides, it could be dangerous for Nick."

"Whatever you say."

Joy was turning cartwheels in my chest, overcoming skepticism and nausea. Maria checked my eyes for sincerity and continued. "You'll have to leave right away. If you stay here, there's too big a chance Drakonakis will drag you in for questioning. We'll get out at the second floor, turn left, take some service stairs down to the side door. There's usually a taxi or two waiting around the back. Then you go straight to Hotel Delfini in Piraeus. No side trips."

"Are you coming?"

"No."

"Piraeus. Hotel Delfini."

The elevator was ascending again, having admitted a middle-aged, soberly dressed businessman on the ground floor. Maria inspected him carefully.

"Take a room there for the night. You're expected. If our friend is having this lobby watched, he won't know you've gone. If he's checking hotel registrations, it won't matter, because the Delfini won't make you fill out a card. You'll get a short visit, either tonight or in the morning, quite early. I can't say exactly when, I just don't know yet. Afterwards, leave right away and return here. Got it?"

"Certainly."

I felt like shouting. Maria the consummate schemer, mistress of emergency, sweeping me up in her plans, if not her arms: only this time, *I'd* be in control. Once I got to Piraeus, once I had Nick again, I'd be able to look after things my own way.

We got out at the second floor.

"I hope you know what you're doing," I said, adding, "my love"—partly to cover my excitement, partly to convey my gratitude, in a self-mocking manner I hope she'd recognize.

She did. "Screw you," she replied.

At the foot of the service stairs, we pushed open a metal door onto the glare outside, emerging into a parallelogram of shade. On the street running behind the hotel, two cabs were waiting. I got inside the first one while Maria spoke to the driver. I wished there were more time for us to talk. I wished even more that she were coming with me.

I leaned out the window and squeezed her hand. She actually held on, actually squeezed back.

"Listen," I told her, rushing to get it all out, "about last night, I mean I was upset about Nick and everything, but that's no excuse, I should never have—"

She was looking hard at me. "You're very different when you drink, you know. I didn't think it mattered once."

"When will we see each other again?"

Her mouth twitched slightly. She compressed her lips, dimpling her chin, then shrugged and stuck her free hand into her pants pocket. "Never, I guess."

The driver, having consulted his city map, was putting the cab in gear. As he pulled away from the curb, our hands were yanked apart.

I stuck my head out the window and looked back at her. She raised her arm, as if signalling the driver to stop, then opened her mouth, but nothing came out. Her raised arm continued upwards into a goodbye wave.

19

The Delfini was on a sidestreet not far from the main harbour in Piraeus, three storeys high, shuttered like a country inn. Its old-fashioned appearance contrasted with the larger, newer buildings surrounding it. A few empty tables sat on the terrace under a luxuriant vine.

I passed through the open doorway to a front desk that doubled as a bar, untended at the moment. Radiant bottles in various stages of consumption lined the glass shelves against a discoloured mirror. As I looked around for a bell to announce my arrival, a stocky, silver-haired gent with a moustache emerged from somewhere in the back, pushing his suspenders up over his shoulders. I'd interrupted his afternoon nap. Inserting himself behind the bar, he nodded gravely and pronounced a rehearsed welcome:

"How are you. Very nice to meet you."

"Fine thanks. How are you?"

That apparently exhausted his English. Uncomfortably, he looked down at the desk. My eyes followed his, coming to rest on a stack of business cards arranged neatly beside an antique cash register: "Hotel 'Delfini', Piraeus, Classe 'C', G. Charalambos, prop." Alongside, there was a smaller pile of guest registration cards; Mr. Charalambos didn't ask me to fill one out.

He made a grimace of apology and said, *"Vous êtes le monsieur canadien?"*

"C'est moi."

"Et vous n'avez pas de bagages, monsieur?"

"Rien. Je pars demain matin."

With my identity and our mode of communication established, Mr. Charalambos became cheerier. *"Eh bien, je vous montre la chambre.*"

I followed him upstairs. It was an eerie sensation, knowing he'd anticipated my arrival. What had Maria told him about me? Was Mr. Charalambos in on her scheme? Did he know something I didn't? Something about Nick?

Room number eight was on the third floor, giving onto the street. Mr. Charalambos showed me in, then hovered mutely in the doorway as if there was something he wanted to tell me but couldn't—perhaps because of the language barrier, or some more sinister reason. Finally inclining his head graciously, he hurried off.

So: this was where I'd see Nick at last! The room was distinctly spartan, bare walls, terracotta tile floor, a scarred night-table with a couple of drawers. Although there was a double bed, it was your basic room for commercial travellers. Queer sort of place for Nick and me to rendezvous. I was beginning to feel like a partner in the *syrtaki*, that stately Greek dance—the guy in the middle of the triangle, hanging on for dear life to handkerchiefs clasped high by his two partners, who initiate all the steps while he merely follows.

As excited as I felt about seeing Nick in the morning, it disturbed me that we had to go to such excessive lengths to meet. Who else was as desperate as I to find him? The ESA, for example? I realized he could be a material witness in their investigation of Yannis Antonopoulos, but still....

But still, they'd killed Yannis, hadn't they?

Then there was Maria's injunction not to press him to explain. What, exactly? What was the secret that everyone was so anxious to keep?

The silence in the room provided no answers. Growing apprehensive again, I opened a pair of louvered shutters closed against the midday heat. They gave onto a pair of long narrow doors with glass panels, then a shallow balcony, little more than a ledge with an iron grille running across it. I opened the doors wide. Below, the grapevine snaked above the terrace; through gaps in the leaves I could see white metal tables and chairs and, beyond, a sidewalk on the opposite side of the street, where a handful of old men were sitting in the open doorway of a café. Two of them were deep into a game of backgammon; the rest sat snoozing in the shade or languidly flipping worry-beads. Here and there across the rooftops a Greek flag waved in the ocean breeze, as if this were a day of celebration.

Looking around to the left, I could see part of the marina, and the outer harbour in the distance. In addition to the usual oil tankers waiting to dock in the inner harbour, a considerable portion of the Greek navy sat at anchor on a sheet of glaring sea. Destroyers of various classes were moored within hailing distance of each other. And in the marina itself, instead of yachts and sailboats with pennants fluttering, squat grey patrol boats and sub-chasers crowded together, looking all the uglier for basking in the Attic light.

I'd never seen so many military craft massed in one place. If the Turkish air force had wanted to stage another Pearl Harbor, they could have accomplished it then and there.

The thought unsettled me. I looked for other signs of war preparedness, but military personnel seemed oddly absent from the scene. Apart from a party of sailors swabbing down the decks of a vessel in the marina, the Greek navy seemed to have gone on siesta. The general air of neglect was reassuring.

I thought of going for a walk, examining the naval activity up close. Then I remembered Costa's caution about being watched, and Maria's insistence not to let anyone know where I was, or that I was seeing Nick. Although it was difficult to put any store in their warnings, I couldn't risk ignoring them: I decided to stay inside. I felt hemmed in, impotent, frustrated. I wasn't used to being under other people's control.

The men at the café across the street seemed blasé about the presence of warships a few hundred yards away. But their heads turned in unison as the loud, high-pitched whine of a motor scooter approached from up the street. It sounded as if something was wrong with the scooter's engine; it was going far too fast. As the driver entered my field of vision, I saw he was an old man wearing a black beret, his chin resting in a peculiar, unnatural position on his chest. With helpless fascination I watched him pass the café at high speed and drive unswervingly into a lamppost.

131

The impact of metal against metal made a sickeningly liquid sound. The scooter lurched sideways onto the sidewalk while the driver pitched forward, his head striking the lamppost full force, then he slid down into the gutter like a marionette whose strings had been cut. His outflung hand came to rest beside his beret.

Gripping the railing, I watched the café patrons suddenly become animated, springing out of their chairs to converge on the prostrate man, to shout at him in a mixture of concern and admonition. They plucked at his clothes, prodded him familiarly, turned his face upwards, remonstrated with him. But nothing did any good.

Other people rushed to the scene from doorways nearby. The crowd grew until I could no longer see the body. People argued over what to do, ignoring the victim altogether. Finally one of the backgammon players dispatched a young waiter for help, and in a moment a little three-wheeled delivery truck arrived, a cross between a scooter and a pick-up, and the body was hoisted off the pavement by two onlookers and unceremoniously dumped into the flatbed behind the driver. When the driver tried to leave for the hospital, his route was blocked by the crowd until they formed an opening to let him through.

With the spectacle over, the crowd dispersed, the street became quiet again. I realized how fast my heart was beating. A few men, perhaps those who'd known the victim, lingered by the lamppost to confer over the broken glass and the remains of the scooter. They stared at a large, dark stain on the asphalt, no doubt impressed—as I was—by how much blood the old man had lost in such a very short time.

I began to feel conspicuous up on my balcony—a voyeur on his perch. No one seemed to have noticed me. I wanted to break through the barrier separating me from the disaster below, to become involved, a participant. When a zealous young waiter arrived with a bucket of water and a broom, I almost yelled at him to leave the evidence alone until the police arrived.

Shaken, I turned back into the room. I closed the shutters behind me. Somehow I was disturbed by something more than witnessing an apparently fatal accident. I had a persistent and furious intuition that the driver had done it to himself—had been responsible for his own destruction.

Of course that was absurd. More likely he'd had a heart attack. I wasn't sure what to make of my anger. I pushed off my shoes and lay down, intending to rest just for a moment, until my head felt better. I wanted to find some way to stitch the weird events of the day into some sort of coherent pattern. I was asleep in less than a minute.

*   *   *

Much later, the dream came. Nick and I were together, trekking along a rocky, barren shore in the north of Scotland. The sea and sky were colourless, without light or promise. We came to a huddle of grey, low-roofed stone cottages beside the snow-rimmed sea. Inside the cottages, raucous parties were going on. Flushed-faced, wild-eyed men and women were drinking out of enormous clay jugs, dancing recklessly to harsh fiddle music. It was all in preparation for the great event, they told us, passing us jugs of vile home-made whisky to drink: the ski-jumping championship, the supreme test of courage and manliness.

Everyone staggered outside into the cold air, carrying skis and ski-poles for the contestants. I realized Nick and I had become separated. I looked around, expecting to see my own father in the crowd, but he was nowhere in sight.

The would-be champions were all virile young men, half-naked even though the air was freezing. One by one they pelted down the frozen hillside at the water's edge, soaring on long pointed skis over the boulders and into the death-bringing sea. Each one vied to be the one who soared highest and farthest before he died.

Finally, amid a great stir of excitement, it was the turn of the people's favourite, the beloved one, the young hero of whom the most was expected. His back was to me, so I couldn't see his face, but I saw his bare upper torso glistening in the dead air, his broad shoulders oiled against the cold and wet. He positioned himself boldly on his skis at the top of the run. Hunched forward, he started downhill in perfect form, swiftly gathering speed, then up and over the upswept lip of the jump in a grand soaring trajectory—until, to moans from the onlookers, his skis became entangled in mid-flight, his grace vanished, and he plummeted straight down, short of the water, onto the rocks.

The spectators clambered over the rocks to see what had become of him. I followed them, shaking with cold, my sense of dread growing uncontrollably because I knew I would discover something terrible.

The tide was out, exposing great expanses of jagged black rock. At last we found his body, lying broken and bloody among the rock pools, as shattered as the bits of skis still attached to his useless feet. His limbs were writhing in slow-motion death agony: his death not glorious, but wasted.

At first I thought, Oh Nick, Nick, pray it's an impostor again! Then my dread dissolved in a flood of relief. When I examined the face more closely, I saw the dying man wasn't Nick at all; it was I, wearing a manic, frozen smile.

20

I woke in darkness, breathing rapidly, the mystery and fear of the dream still upon me. Sitting up fully dressed, I gulped mouthfuls of close, dry air and struggled to remember where I was. Nearby, someone was playing bouzouki music—God, it was loud.

I pulled open the balcony shutters. Voices flooded in. The Delfini's terrace, so quiet earlier in the day, had become transformed while I slept into a carnival—people eating and drinking and laughing under electric lights, children shrieking, adults shouting to be heard above music coming from speakers hidden somewhere in the grape arbour. I caught glimpses of people below through the gaps in the vine, heard the roar of traffic from nearby streets.

Abruptly an amplified male voice broke into the soundscape: a frantic harangue in rapid Greek, growing louder as a Volkswagen Beetle with a loudspeaker on its roof moved up the street. The voice switched into German, then English, just as the car drew level with the hotel: "Looking for good times? Good music? Good wine? Come to Nikos' Place! We're open till the wee hours and we got the best souvlaki, the best bouzouki, the best dancing in Piraeus! Nikos' Place, the mos' fun nightclub in town!"

A dog barked in reply, equally frantic, and the voice started all over again in Greek. The little car passed out of sight, followed by a giant empty tourbus coasting past, whose driver serenaded the diners with a musical fanfare on his horn. They laughed, while somebody yelled something good-naturedly at the driver.

Somehow the cacophony was exhilarating. I felt safer now, less conspicuous—the carnival atmosphere a cover for my alien presence. I also felt rested for the first time since leaving home, and what's more, free to ignore Maria's and Costa's warnings. I decided to go downstairs for something to eat.

The terrace gleamed unnaturally under strings of bare lightbulbs. I entertained a half-conscious hope that Nick might be waiting for me at one of the tables, but there was no sign of him. If he'd arrived while I was asleep, Mr. Charalambos would have sent him straight up to my room.

A dark, curly-headed young man in an open-necked shirt with a gold chain at his throat rushed past on his way inside, his arms full of dirty plates, and grinned at me; he bore a distinct resemblance to Mr. Charalambos.

"Good evening! How you doing?" he shouted above the music.

Feeling less incognito, I sat down at the only free table. The other patrons looked like locals: well-heeled, well-fed couples drinking beer, the beverage of the middle class, instead of wine; a family with several kids; two guys yukking it up with ties askew, bank clerks or civil servants on a boys' night out. The exceptions were a short-haired blond man and woman in their late twenties, Scandinavian or German, so alike it was impossible to tell if they were lovers or siblings. Two empty retsina bottles sat on their table alongside a third, already half-empty. Despite all the wine they'd drunk, this couple didn't look nearly as happy as the long table full of young men sitting next to them, several of whom ogled the woman mercilessly while she studiously ignored them.

There were about a dozen young men, sailors by the look of them, or labourers, obviously regulars at the Delfini from their familiarity with the young waiter. The odd thing was the way they were all dressed—in black jerseys and pants, almost a kind of uniform. The waiter was serving them two huge platters of fried smelts. Accepting an offered cigarette, he lit up and strolled over to where I was sitting.

"Karamanlis on TV tonight," he explained affably. "Big night."

"Oh, of course." I'd forgotten. "What do you think he'll say?"

Pleased to be asked his opinion, he smiled, smoke encircling his black curls. "Bad for the Turks. Greeks won' take it lying down. You will see. Maybe war! I don' know."

I tried not to look too skeptical. He was in a hell of a good humour. "Can I get something to eat first?"

He laughed, patting my shoulder reassuringly. "I fix you up. My name is Dino, okay? My mother is cooking some very, very nice *barbounia*. Or if you prefer, a combinated plate— fish, other fish. Or we have entrecôte, lamb chops, *keftedes*. What you like?"

Barbounia, I remembered, were red mullet. I ordered some with salad and a bottle of retsina. Dino collected plates from the other tables before heading back to the kitchen, his gold chain gleaming, cigarette bobbing at anchor in the corner of his mouth. Like his father, he'd been prepared for my arrival.

I was feeling something I hadn't felt for a long time, a sensation familiar from previous visits to Greece—an ineffable sense of comfort, of rightness, at home in my skin. It came from Dino's warm and unguarded welcome. Hard to imagine Anglo-Saxons acting like that towards some foreigner they'd never set eyes on before. Maria had possessed that same quality: a powerful part of her attraction. In the old days, she'd made me feel good about who and where I was. Happy, I think the word is. She and Dino were brother and sister under the skin.

After he'd brought my meal, Dino shut off the bouzouki tape. The atmosphere on the terrace turned expectant, and he brought an antique television set outside and started tuning it. A milky-white image materialized, accompanied by hysterical commercials that sounded like announcements for World War Three.

There was a brief on-air silence, followed by a funereal gentleman who frowned at the camera while speaking at great length, followed by a still of the Greek flag and the playing of the national anthem. The Delfini's patrons shifted their chairs for a better view. Finally the screen dissolved to a long shot: Prime Minister Karamanlis sitting stiffly at a desk, waiting for his cue, sheets of paper lying in front of him. As the camera did a slow zoom to The Leader, an invisible but palpable line of demarcation was drawn between the Greeks and non-Greeks on the terrace. I was intruding on a family occasion.

In crisp, dry cadences, Karamanlis began to speak. Everything about him was austere, his eyebrows, his pallbearer's suit, his aristocratic yet ascetic features. He looked considerably older than the portraits around town would suggest; Michaelis was practically a young man by comparison. Karamanlis' personal authority was all the more powerful for his years of self-imposed exile in Paris. Having denied himself influence and homeland so long, he'd now returned to claim his due, to set things right.

He spoke like a patriarch instructing a somewhat backward flock, and I caught references to the peace talks going on in Geneva among Greece, Turkey, and Britain, the three guarantors of Cypriot independence. But the audience on the terrace became restless; they were getting a lecture in political science instead of a call to arms against the infidel.

As if sensing their disappointment, Karamanlis heated things up. Some harsh words for the U.S. drew whoops from the lads, applause from the older folks; I gathered he was threatening the Americans' use of their naval bases in Piraeus and Crete. At last he became impassioned, a commander-in-chief exhorting his troops. Shouts of support from the terrace: *now* he was sticking it to the Turks!

Finally Karamanlis switched to a conciliatory, statesman-like tone, demonstrating his reasonableness and generosity, confident the world could see the innate justice of his position. Clearly his talk wasn't just for domestic consumption: he was sending a signal to the Powers, as they're known in Greece, but especially to Mr. Kissinger, or whoever was actually running the White House at the moment, that they'd have to reckon with him.

When Karamanlis vanished from the screen, the Delfini's patrons erupted into a standing ovation. Dino turned the tape player back on, and a new piece of music drowned out the continued blaring of the TV—the fierce, blood-curdling anthem of Greek Resistance from the Second World War, sung in a swaggering baritone accompanied by the bowing of a high-pitched Cretan *lyra*. The young men began singing along at the tops of their lungs.

An extraordinary gaiety now gripped the terrace. People sang, interrupted their singing to talk, to debate what Karamanlis had said, then resumed singing once more. Only the blond foreigners and I sat in silence.

Dino strode over, sweeping me up in a dazzling grin.

"You understan' what Karamanlis say? Greece will never forget the Cyprus. Turks must go home or else! But he also say Greeks want the peace. Turks, do they? He don' know." Dino shrugged interrogatively, raising his black eyebrows Groucho-style.

"What if they don't?" I said.

"Then war, I guess!"

I nodded slowly, resisting his ebullience. "Is Michaelis going to speak too?"

Dino's grin grew even more knowing. "Ah, you know Michaelis, eh? Sure, he will speak. Maybe tomorrow. But he will agree to Karamanlis. It is the only thing possible. Greece gotta be strong! Well, see you later."

Dino rejoined his friends, and in a moment three of them started dancing. As I sat watching them, I thought how, if Greece gotta be strong, then Michaelis had very little latitude to dissent from Karamanlis' position. In fact, from what Costa had told me earlier that day (it seemed ages ago now), Michaelis' own position was going to be even more belligerent. The Turks had been the enemy from time immemorial; no amount of Western influence or socialist philosophy or intellectual wisdom was going to change that.

Eventually one of the young men, clearly very drunk, stood to dance and gestured to the others to join in. They all refused, egging him on to perform solo. There was a tinge of malice to their teasing—perhaps this one fancied himself a great dancer. But the ponderous solemnity of his first slow, tremulous steps didn't inspire confidence. Abruptly, he bent towards the floor, his arm making a downwards swoop that threatened to be his last, yet somehow he managed to keep his balance, restoring himself to an upright position—then repeated the manoeuvre, just to prove it wasn't a fluke.

"*Yasu, Stephano!*" his friends called out.

They were impressed in spite of themselves. They studied Stephano's feet, to judge his balance more than his technique. Finally, unwilling to abandon him to possible humiliation, two of the young men joined him and linked hands in a chain—but in that chain, Stephano remained the leader, the star. Accepting his partners with regal aloofness, he danced on, head held disdainfully high, staring upwards at something only he could see.

The dancing continued for several numbers. Stephano was persuaded to retire, and other patrons joined in, including a plump, middle-aged couple. The blond foreigners studied the whole spectacle with immense seriousness, working their way methodically through their fourth bottle of retsina, still not speaking or cracking a smile or even looking at each other. The male and female singers wailed on, hurling their nasal love-calls at each other, their bitter accusatory laments, their agonized moans of pain and lust. Each song seemed faster and more reckless than the one before, urging the sweating dancers on to new heights.

Suddenly there was a sharp crash. The dancing stopped. One of the bank clerks dove prudently to the floor—no doubt a result of military training. Everyone else gaped, in variations of astonishment or outrage, at the blond couple.

Mortified, the woman didn't know where to look—she'd have preferred to drop straight through the floor, anything to disappear from the staring. Her companion, on the other hand, appeared positively delighted with himself. Although reddening with self-consciousness and alcohol, he was beaming broadly at the white shards of crockery lying like shrapnel at the dancers' feet: he'd performed the very ritual that *Zorba the Greek* and out-of-date tourist guides had informed him was the traditional way of showing one's enthusiasm for good Greek dancing and good Greek high spirits. He'd smashed a dinner plate on the floor.

Slowly, obscurely, he began to wonder if he'd miscalculated. Or had he? In spite of the shocked stares, the flight of the middle-aged couple back to their table, the young men revived the dancing with greater abandon than ever. They shouted fiercely at the foreigners, gesturing to them to join in, and the big guy, looking relieved, started to rise until his companion pulled him back by the wrist.

Even the forgotten Stephano rose from his place of retirement. Seizing an empty plate, he made a great show of hoisting it high above his head with both hands before triumphantly dashing it to the floor beside the dancers.

This was too much for Mr. Charalambos. At the sound of the first plate breaking, he'd appeared in the entrance looking alarmed. Now he was beside himself. He rushed in to quell the uprising: it was no longer merely a question of drunken foreigners who didn't know any better. Lunging at Dino, he grabbed him by the shoulders with both hands and manhandled him into the dancers' midst, forcing them to stop once again.

Charalambos berated the lads with real ferocity. He had to shout to be heard above the music, eyes flashing, silver moustache bristling, arms and saliva flying, and I could make out the words "foreigners" and "police". He'd had nothing like this in his establishment, I imagined, for seven years — not since the Colonels had outlawed the breaking of plates in public places because it symbolized defiance of their regime.

Mr. Charalambos wasn't about to repeal the law unilaterally. Ignorant tourists were one thing, his son and his friends entirely another. The junta might no longer be in power, but somebody was, and Charalambos was damned if he was going to give them an excuse to close him down.

Dino argued gamely with his father but knew it was no good; he was already reaching for a broom. The lads returned to their table, laughing among themselves to save face, to show they didn't give a damn. Eventually they all left together to go somewhere, and the incident was over.

I sat on while Charalambos and a young woman cleared the tables, and most of the guests collected themselves to depart. I needed movement — a little exercise to work the anxiety of waiting out of my system. I walked off the terrace and into the street, passing the scene of the afternoon's accident. I looked for the bloodstain on the pavement, but couldn't see it in the dark.

*　*　*

After a few blocks I caught the smell of the sea. I turned up a sidestreet and emerged into a large open area giving onto the main harbour, where two white ships were moored close together along the quay, their bridges awash with light: ferries getting up steam to leave for the islands at midnight. Both were taking on passengers, who straggled up the gangways carrying parcels and shopping bags, trophies of their visit to the capital.

Farther along, I came to an unobstructed view of the inner harbour: cranes, warehouses, oil tanks, barges, all spangled with lights reflected in the black water. I smelled the pungency of diesel oil, heard the distant thrumming of a ship's engines. There was something festive in the air—as if a giant waterborne party were about to begin. And indeed, something did appear to be happening. A crowd was milling excitedly around a parking area. Curious, I walked over.

There must have been forty or fifty young men there, all wearing dark shirts and pants like the ones at the Delfini; only now they'd added red sashes to their waists, a folkloric touch, so perhaps they belonged to some youth group or patriotic association. Bottles were being passed around, interfering with sporadic, half-serious attempts to form up into marching order. Nobody seemed in charge. Some older men hung about looking on enviously and shouting gruff, good-humoured encouragement, like supporters of the home team before a game.

Two teenage boys were struggling with wooden poles supporting either end of a huge white banner. It was so heavy it kept sagging in the middle, obscuring a slogan written in large black capitals. A chant started up, evidently in the words of the slogan, as if that would impart new strength to the bearers and make the banner straighten out. I tried to catch the words of the chant. One was *junta*. Another was *megali*, meaning "big", but the rest was lost on me.

Far from being black-shirted fascists, then, as I'd briefly surmised, these young men were about to stage some sort of anti-junta demonstration—a retroactive protest, as it were, against the vanished regime. I couldn't really blame them for waiting until the danger of being gunned down was past. Somebody shouted a denunciation of Kissinger, and a few others joined in, trying it out for size.

They were drowned out by exultant cheers from a larger group on the far side of the crowd, where an American flag had been set on fire. The sight of the burning Stars and Stripes incited howls of delight. People leaped dangerously close to the flames, sending patches of burning cloth flaring up into the night sky, vying for a chance to wave the flagstaff back and forth.

Help arrived for the drooping banner. Someone had located a tree branch shaped like a diviner's rod, and he positioned the fork against the bottom of the banner, pushing upwards while two fresh volunteers took over the poles. Obediently the banner straightened out, and I could read the entire slogan:

JUNTA, NATO, CIA, MEGALI PROTISIA.

From the chanting, I could tell that "*NATO*" was pronounced with a short "a", while "*CIA*" was pronounced "SEE-A", rhyming with "*PROTISIA*"—whatever that meant.

Finally the column was ready to march. Out of the corner of my eye, I barely noticed a marcher detaching himself from the rest, moving in my direction. Then I realized he was coming straight at me. In surprise, I turned to see what he wanted, belatedly aware it wasn't anything friendly. Simultaneously, I heard and felt a hot gob of spit strike my left cheek.

I stared in disbelief at the spitter. It was Stephano, the dancer from the Delfini.

Stephano pointed a finger at me and screamed something, in the same tone as the denouncer of Kissinger. I didn't need to understand exactly what he was saying: it was enough to hear the word "*Amerikis*". This brought the march to a halt. Everyone was turning in my direction. Jesus. Both disgusted and afraid, I wiped the spit off my face with the back of my hand.

Another marcher joined Stephano. Luckily he was younger, and considerably smaller, but probably just as drunk. He was trying to look manful and full of hatred. I was the Antichrist. With a certain detachment, I wondered how I could possibly have gotten myself into a situation where I was so absurdly outnumbered.

A third guy, bigger than the first two, ran over quickly to join them. Here goes, I thought, bracing myself for their assault, wondering if I had any boxing skills left from my university days, adrenalin pumping through my system every which way. My brain was trying to keep track of their sizes and positions, their distance from me (for all the good it would do), wondering how quick their reactions would be, and whether they'd be at all discouraged by my superior size or by an aggressive gesture, when the third young man grabbed Stephano by the back of the neck and pushed him effortlessly to his knees, possibly exerting pressure on some nerve in the drunken boy's neck. Then he turned in a graceful fluid motion and cracked the other one across the cheek with the back of his hand.

It took me a second to recognize my benefactor: Dino Charalambos, disguised by a wide black sweatband concealing his forehead and curls.

After a thorough dressing-down from Dino, and without another glance at me, Stephano scrambled back to his feet and slunk off to his place among the marchers. The other boy followed suit without needing to be told.

I was panting, trying to catch my breath. I needed to slow my heart down. I felt a mixture of relief and embarrassment—in a sense, it was my uncalled-for presence that had been responsible for this incident.

Dino looked me up and down. "You okay?" he said anxiously.

"Yeah. Great. Thanks."

"*Theos mou*," he muttered. "Those guys don' know a thing." He spoke softly, not wanting to be heard speaking English. "They drink too much, they go crazy, they say you're American. A spy on us."

"Oh."

"I tell them you're not American, you're Canadian. A friend. You stay at the Delfini. You're cool. Right?"

"Right."

Limp with gratitude, I wondered in which American ports Dino had picked up his English. Below the headband, his handsome face was suffused with sweat. It wouldn't have been easy for him to defend me; but he'd upheld the honour of his father's establishment, his family's hospitality. Now he was agitated, an actor made up for his part, impatient to get back on stage.

"Sure you okay?" he asked again.

"Absolutely. Thanks for what you did. Now please, go ahead, don't worry." I gestured towards the others. As he turned away, I called after him, "Oh Dino — just one thing."

"Yes?"

"What does *protisia* mean?"

He frowned and said, "Betray? Betray-al? Something like that."

*　　*　　*

Dino took his place behind the standard-bearer at the front of the line, giving me a reassuring nod as the marchers moved off. Now they started to chant with real fervour.

"*Kas-tri!*" a few voices shouted bravely. They were answered by "*Ka-ra-man-lis!*" in greater numbers. Several marchers stared at me with open curiosity, not entirely unfriendly, as they passed.

I watched them leave the square, followed by their hangers-on, then enter the first street leading into the heart of Piraeus. Passing drivers honked their horns in support.

I was the only person left in the parking lot. Normally I was a big fan of Greek demos, but I'd seen all I wanted of this one. Realizing I'd been away from the hotel far longer than I'd intended, I walked back in the direction of the Delfini.

I passed a young couple whispering and giggling under a basket of flowers hanging from a lamppost, a sailor and his girl, enjoying the freedom of the night. Two hookers in tight dresses lounged and smoked on a street corner.

Then, within a block of the hotel, I saw Nick.

He was up ahead, strolling beside a slim, much shorter young man. The two of them were conversing intently. My body and soul filled with excitement — yet I didn't want to alarm him, scare him off, so I didn't call out his name or run to him, as I was tempted to, just quickened my pace, and in a moment I was within five yards of them. They walked straight past the hotel entrance. Intending to call them back, I came up close behind them, so close I practically inserted myself between them — and by then I could catch their conversation, and it was in Greek.

Startled by my intrusion, "Nick" looked over his shoulder. I saw the resemblance was completely superficial. Feeling a complete fool, I excused myself and turned away, trembling a little, and went back to the hotel.

I stood outside the entrance for a moment, collecting myself. The terrace was empty now, silent; a bare lightbulb threw vine-shadows across empty tables. The front door, although closed, was unlocked. If the real Nick had arrived in my absence, he could have gone inside to wait, or could have rung and asked for my room.

Upstairs, however, the room was unoccupied.

As I struggled to get to sleep during the next several hours, I wondered repeatedly where Nick was spending the night, and with whom.

21

U nsure when Nick would be arriving, I rose with the sun. Downstairs I encountered Mr. Charalambos, already up and about. You could tell he liked that early hour. Chatting cheerfully in French, he offered yogurt, eggs, and coffee; I requested all three.

I could hear the port waking in the distance, but the street in front of the Delfini remained perfectly still, imitating a country village. Adding to the illusion, Mr. Charalambos brought thick warm slabs of fresh bread accompanied by pots of sweet butter and strong-tasting Hymettus honey, and a glass bowl of sheep's-milk yogurt, thick and creamy under its wrinkled skin. When I'd eaten the yogurt, he served an excellent golden omelette floating on a pond of olive oil.

After a *metrio*, I strolled down the street to a corner kiosk already doing a brisk business in cigarettes. A large black telephone sat on the counter beside stacks of movie magazines. The phone's presence made me feel less isolated; I could use it to call Helen Diamantides after Nick arrived, letting her know everything was all right after all.

I asked for an *Athens News*. The proprietress rolled it up for me before taking my money, and I didn't unroll it right away, because I wanted to save it for reading on the terrace of the Delfini. The morning still hadn't turned uncomfortably hot. It would be a pleasure to sit in the shade under the grapevine and read and look forward to seeing Nick.

Resuming my seat, I opened the paper, expecting to read about Karamanlis' televised address. Instead, the headline announced Richard Nixon's resignation.

Like most people, I'd assumed all through Watergate that Nixon had been lying. The only surprise was that he'd finally owned up to it. Sipping a glass of water that Charalambos brought, I read about Nixon's last hours as president: his statement to the American people, his heart-to-heart with his family, his final words to his staff, what he'd said to his Eisenhower son-in-law, what he'd eaten for breakfast. In a photograph taken outside the helicopter waiting to whisk him away to exile in California, he looked as brazenly smug and self-righteous as ever, in spite of the enormity of what he'd admitted. It was extraordinary: he still seemed to expect people to believe in his good intentions, his inner rectitude, no matter how deceitful his actions. Why did I feel a glimmer of sympathy for him?

It was like news from another planet. I devoured it eagerly, hungry for every scrap of information from a world that, as sterile and materialistic as it might be, was at least familiar — still ruled, at least in theory, by values of responsibility and justice and retribution.

A report of Karamanlis' television address stretched across the bottom of page one; it confirmed that Dino's little précis of the speech had been quite accurate. The only fresh development was the dispatch of an American envoy to shuttle between Ankara and Athens. He'd be reporting to Secretary of State Kissinger and the new President Ford, a title that would take some getting used to.

There was a related story on page three. It struck me as even more astounding than Nixon's resignation:

"Socialist leader Michaelis Kastri, still denied the use of state television, held a press conference last night after Prime Minister Karamanlis spoke to the nation."

Michaelis hadn't held back. I read how he'd condemned the prime minister for failing to purge the officer corps, for failing to lift martial law, for failing to launch an investigation into the Polytechnic massacre. It was all consistent with his earlier pronouncements on these matters. But then Michaelis accused Karamanlis of "moral and political weakness", meaning softness on both the Turks and the Americans. He demanded to know why the prime minister hadn't yet called up the military reserves, why he wasn't putting the armed forces back on war alert. The CIA had supported the military takeover in 1967, Michaelis charged, and now

Kissinger was backing the Turks over Cyprus, preparing to sell out Greek interests yet again. What was Karamanlis going to do about it?

Michaelis' solution was brutally simple: Karamanlis should abrogate the Americans' leases on their Greek naval bases—leases that were worthless anyway, having been signed by the junta—and assert Greek sovereignty once and for all by mobilizing troops and preparing to send them, if necessary, to Cyprus.

Jesus: it would be an act of all-out war. No doubt about that. It could only expand the fighting beyond Cyprus to engulf the mainland and the cities, the entire population of Greece, and to what purpose?

I kept seeing a mental picture of Yannis lying bloody and broken in his cell. The excesses of Greek politics had already resulted in one young man's death by torture; now they were turning my humanitarian friend into a jingoist. How could Michaelis bring himself to urge such a reckless policy? Had Costa advised it? How could such a people ever govern themselves democratically, rationally?

I gulped water, telling myself not to overvalue reason, or underestimate passion, in politics. Yet Michaelis had so much to offer his country—his brilliance, his breadth of learning and experience, his compassion. He should have been helping to make Greece saner, not more violent.

Involuntarily I began to rationalize, to search for explanations. Perhaps Michaelis' rhetoric shouldn't be taken literally; perhaps it had an ulterior motive. It might be a way of protecting himself against the ESA, for example. Costa's version of the ESA's machinations came back to me: if they did succeed in discrediting Michaelis, linking him to some trumped-up conspiracy, they'd be able to raise the spectre of left-wing revolution. So he might simply be heading them off—coming across as a zealous super-patriot, a stauncher nationalist and enemy of the Turks than they were. I thought of other interpretations, each cleverer than the last. Still. Any way you looked at it, it was lunacy.

Speculating along these lines, I sat and watched the shadows retreat to the base of the walls as the sun rose higher and hotter. My good mood of the early morning had also retreated.

I told myself to keep my hopes up, not to jump to unwarranted conclusions. It was still early, wasn't it? Nick would get there: it was just a matter of time.

"A visit in the morning," Maria had said. Then she'd added, "quite early."

I thought how Nick had "appeared" to me three times on the previous day. First there had been the voice on Costa's tape; then the dream of the self-immolating heroes on the Scottish coast; and finally the false identification on the street at the end of the evening. Each "visit" had been less real than the one before. The recording of Nick's voice, for all its staged quality, was by far the best—perhaps the only—piece of evidence to support Maria and Costa's claim that he really was in Athens, alive.

When ten o'clock arrived, then eleven, and eleven-thirty, my remaining faith frayed to the breaking point. At noon, it snapped. It no longer seemed possible to deny the fact that Nick wasn't coming. I could spend the rest of my life sitting there and never see him again.

I was angry. Once again I'd been manipulated by Maria. Clearly she'd sent me to Piraeus just to get me out of the way.

Then anger was replaced by fear. An immense and paralysing anguish stole over me. All my optimism, my marshalled hope, mustered to attention since yesterday afternoon, was in danger of collapsing like a soldier left out too long on parade. Everything I'd done since visiting Drakonakis' prison two days earlier suddenly seemed futile and absurd, a series of empty gestures. In the absence of any other evidence, it seemed possible that Yannis might have been telling me the simple truth about Nick after all.

And yet I still couldn't believe Maria would lie to me, send me up a blind alley in hope, while knowing Nick was dead. My mind scrambled desperately over alternative explanations of what must have happened.

He'd tried to get to the Delfini but had been intercepted on the way.

By whom?

The ESA.

The Tourist Police.

One of Michaelis' people.

Or he'd come to some kind of harm. An accident?

Or merely a bad case of nerves, a panic attack. Why? Not wanting to face up to me. To explain himself. Yes, that was plausible: he simply wanted nothing more to do with me.

At that point, Mr. Charalambos came outside. He'd changed into a dark suit, and could have been on his way to see his banker or his priest. He walked past me across the terrace, tipping a black-brimmed hat in my direction.

I looked hard at him — a successful father, in my eyes — for some sort of sign, some clue as to what I should do in my desolation. He caught my gaze. Although he didn't say a word, his forehead furrowed in a frown of alarm, and he made a grimace of warning before hurrying off. Whatever you do, he seemed to be saying, don't remain here.

After a decent interval, I followed him down the street, past the kiosk, and around the corner. I wasn't sure why I was following him; but it felt better than passively sitting and waiting. Passing several blocks of mixed offices and shops, he disappeared around another corner. By then I'd come to a small establishment renting cars. I made a quick decision and went inside.

From a personable young woman who spoke excellent English, I rented a white, much-driven, but apparently sound Renault 10. She had me fill out a form, took an imprint from my VISA card, handed me the keys, and wished me a happy holiday in Greece.

Still acting on instinct, I drove back to the Delfini. I'd begun to worry in case Nick had arrived in my absence and gone away again. But at the front desk Dino, who had just risen after his exertions of the previous night, assured me I'd had no visitors or phone calls.

I asked him for the bill, and he seemed reluctant to charge me; after rooting around laboriously in his father's account book, he quoted an absurdly low amount for the room, less than a quarter of the rate I was paying at the Olympic Palace. I handed him what I thought the room was worth, suggesting he give some of it to the maid, if any, or keep it himself.

"Want a drink?" he asked. "It's on the house."

From among the aperitifs and ouzos and Greek brandies lined up on the shelf behind him, a brand of Scotch with which I'd once been intimate flaunted itself at me. This was my cue, then — my signal to throw it all away, to throw myself, like Aegeus, into the sea of drunkenness.

Like hell. Anger over my situation reasserted itself. Instead of anesthetizing it in alcohol, I allowed the anger to take hold. You have a right, it told me, you do not have to subdue this feeling. *Somebody* has been lying to you, screwing you around. Somebody you trusted.

I told Dino no thanks and goodbye. I started towards my rented car but, feeling one last qualm, decided to wait on the terrace just a few minutes longer, just in case I was being overly impatient.

Even the shade was unpleasantly hot now. My eyes, my brain, began to hurt from the incessant glare. At one o'clock, with nothing to show for my stay in Piraeus, a total duration of nearly twenty-four hours, I threw myself behind the wheel of the car, twisted the key in the ignition, and started towards Kalamaki.

22

It was already siesta when I reached Maria's neighbourhood. The Americans' villas lay deep in the shade of their pines and eucalyptus, like ships at anchor. Turning the corner, I parked in front of the little house, which was baking in the full sun like a pot in a kiln. Maria had said she often returned home at lunchtime for a swim and a nap, and as I knocked on her door I prayed this was one of those days.

"Come in, then."

She stood aside to let me enter, locking the door quickly behind me. She was wearing a man's white cotton shirt, the tails hanging outside an old pair of jeans cut off at the thighs. Her shutters were closed. The interior seemed cave-like, preternaturally dim after the brightness outside.

We both stood motionless in the hallway, speechless, staring at each other while my eyes adjusted.

I said, "I trusted you."

"You had no reason not to."

"But?"

"But what did you say to Costa that got him so upset?"

"*Costa's* upset?"

"He's practically hysterical."

"Does that explain why Nick didn't show up?"

"Costa refused to let him go."

"Since when does Costa have all this control?"

She continued looking closely at me, seeming calmer, reassured. "You still don't understand, do you?"

I placed a hand carefully, unthreateningly, on her wrist. She let it remain. Being in physical contact made it all a little easier.

"Last night, I practically got lynched for being an American. So I wasn't *completely* surprised when Nick didn't show up this morning—but no, I don't understand. And I'm sick to death of not understanding. That's why I've come here. To you, my love."

"Don't say that."

She turned away into her kitchen. I followed helplessly. The old bond between us was truly terrible, I felt, like joined flesh, like a sentence. Neither of us seemed able to break it.

We sat down on opposite sides of her wooden kitchen table. The cool, moist air was a refuge against the implacable heat outside. Dropping my suit jacket onto an empty chair, I examined the brown depths of Maria's eyes, the bronze flesh of her mouth, the pale flesh of her earlobe pierced with a single gold stud. She seemed to examine the table's scarred surface for a time, then looked up at me quickly from beneath her fall of hair.

"When Costa found out Nick was going to see you, he panicked. He thinks you're co-operating with the ESA. Is it true?"

"No. Believe me."

"Well, he's convinced you're going to ruin everything. He's forbidden Nick even to say goodbye to you. And of course he's furious with me."

"What makes Costa so paranoid?"

"Michaelis."

"Michaelis doesn't want me to see my own son?"

"He's still very unsure of himself here. He doesn't know who to trust. Except for Costa. He trusts Costa to take care of things—to take whatever steps are in his best interests."

"Including keeping me away from Nick." I shook my head in disbelief. "I still don't get it."

"All right. Keep this absolutely between us, or I'll be in very serious trouble."

She studied me the whole time she spoke, as if her brain were weighing something very different from what she was saying. I got the feeling, as she warmed to her tale, that she was enjoying it.

"Just before I left Toronto, Michaelis made me an offer.

At first I couldn't believe it, he knew my opinion of him. But he was serious: he needed a liaison with the Left, what was left of it, in Athens. He wanted me to learn whatever I could — the different factions in the resistance, the emerging leaders, what was left of his father's old party, everything. He needed to build bridges. I'd be a sort of envoy, someone who'd seen him in Toronto and could spread the word he'd be returning."

"I'm surprised this attracted you."

"I was skeptical at first. Totally. But eventually he persuaded me. You know how he can be. We talked about the structural problems of the Left, the eternal bickering, the impossibility of getting power without a common front, et cetera, we agreed on all that. And in a way, I was flattered to be asked. Besides, it was my ticket home. Away from you."

I didn't say anything. Michaelis had never mentioned a word of this.

"Once I got here, I found no resistance movement to speak of. The Left was in total disarray, the leaders were in prison, everyone was demoralized and apathetic.

"But around the end of last year, I began hearing strange things about Alekos Panagoulis. He'd gone to Italy after being released by the ESA. I thought maybe he'd gone bonkers over there — he was supposed to be organizing an urban guerrilla network in Athens by long distance. It would be divided into cells and called 'The People's Army of Resistance'. The crazy thing was, each cell contained exactly one person. It sounded like a mad joke.

"Then his handbills started appearing. They had headlines like 'The Absolute Necessity for Armed Resistance against the Tyrants'. People came across them on sidewalks, in Omonia Square, on buses, café tables, they were all over the Parthenon, translated into Italian and German and signed 'Alexander Panagoulis' in his funny handwriting. He'd had them printed in Rome and smuggled into Athens, along with rubber stamps for printing more."

"Bizarre."

"I thought so. I doubted that kind of tactic would do any good. Some of my friends disagreed, though — they said

Panagoulis raised their morale. Then he really impressed me
—he smuggled *himself* into Athens. He just flew in on a
regular flight from Rome, carrying a Swedish passport
and wearing some ridiculous wig. He'd counted on the
airport police being too stupid to recognize him. He was
right. They got a lot tougher after that. Anyhow, not bad, I
thought. That's when I met him."

"How?"

Maria looked pleased with herself. As she leaned across
the table towards me, her breasts shifted subtly inside her
cotton shirt. She pressed them against her brown forearms.
Catching the warm, baked-bread scent of her, I tried to
concentrate on some relatively unerotic zone—her seamless
forehead, the army of grey slowly invading her hair.

"A friend of mine was hiding him for a night. Sleeping
with him in the process, of course, she's a complete slut.
Anyway, I'd coached her in what to tell him—that I could
be trusted, that I wanted to help him in any way I could. I
figured it was important for Michaelis to know whatever he
was up to.

"I went to my friend's flat and she introduced us. Panagoulis is quite crazy, but he has this incredible animal energy.
It must be what allowed him to survive the torture."

"Did you sleep with him too?"

"Don't be ridiculous. He tried, of course, but when he
saw there was no point he got serious. He actually told me his
strategy for eliminating the Colonels: that was the point of
his 'People's Army'. Afterwards he asked me questions about
what he'd said, like a professor giving an oral.

"I knew he had complete contempt for Michaelis, so I
had to sound like I did too. It wasn't hard. Finally Alekos
asked if I'd be prepared to act as a contact for him: provide
his supporters with a safe house, get them money or supplies
when they needed it, that kind of thing. So I agreed. I told
him *my* house was safe, he'd just better tell his people not to
come here if they're being watched.

"He went back to Rome, and I heard nothing more for
months. Then the Colonels made their move on Cyprus.
That jarred Alekos into action: he was convinced Ioannides

156

and the rest of them were insane—by provoking war with Turkey, they were going to destroy Greece. So now was the time to activate the People's Army of Resistance."

I interrupted. "Why do I get the feeling you're stalling me again?"

"Po-po-po. Don't worry, I'm coming to Nick."

I closed my eyes and listened as she continued.

"Panagoulis had plenty of weapons hidden around the city, but he needed someone he could trust to do the job."

Suddenly my eyes were wide open. "What job?"

"To assassinate Ioannides."

There it was again. Trust the Greeks to go overboard, to seize on the wildest extreme, the ultimate madness, the crazy melodrama of murder.

"He'd have preferred to do it himself, I think. He honestly didn't want to put anyone else at risk. But he was afraid he'd be recognized before he got close enough. Ioannides had bodyguards all over the place. So it had to be one of the 'cells'."

I shook my head. "I can't believe Nick got mixed up in this."

"Nick was still in Rome then—just seeing the sights, hanging around the student cafés. He met a Greek student and they became lovers. She was one of Panagoulis' acolytes —he collects them like flies—and she told Nick about the People's Army. He expressed solidarity with the cause, so eventually, through this girl, Alekos let it be known there was something Nick could contribute to the struggle."

"His life?"

"His passport."

"Oh, right. Why not?"

"Jim, I think there's something you should realize about Nick. He wanted *terribly* to get involved. To take a stand, to commit himself. He's incredibly idealistic, you know. Sure, maybe he was pressured by the Panagoulis people, maybe he just wanted to prove himself to the girl, but I believe he cared. I really do."

"I have no trouble believing that. Anyway, it was the least he could do."

She gave me a sharp glance, pausing a moment before continuing. "Alekos had chosen the 'cell' to do the job—Yannis Antonopoulos, a law student. Yannis had the conviction to commit murder, his best friend had been blown apart by a tank at the Polytechnic. But first he had to be trained—by Panagoulis personally. Rather than risk another sneak into Athens, Alekos decided to bring Yannis to Rome. The problem was how to do this and then get Yannis quickly back to Athens, without attracting attention. The solution was to turn him into a foreign tourist. An innocent."

"To turn him into Nick."

Maria went on, not missing a beat. "Yannis was unusually tall for a Greek—the same height and build as Nick. And nearly the right age, give or take a couple of years. Through the girlfriend, Panagoulis provided Nick with a ticket to Athens, with instructions about how to get his passport to Yannis."

"And Nick was sent to you." I said this instinctively, not reasoning it out; and with a kind of wonderment.

Maria leaned back in her chair, watching me. "Exactly. I was as amazed as you are. Nick is the only contact Panagoulis ever sent me."

My heart was racing. "Did he remember you?"

"He didn't seem to at first. He thought there was something familiar about me, that's all. Even when I reminded him, he didn't know who I was to you—just that I'd stayed on your sofa one night in Toronto. That stray cat coming in from the rain."

"Jesus."

She gave me another look.

"A few days earlier, Costa had wired me some money from Toronto. It was supposed to be for a 'courier'. Well, the courier turned out to be Nick: he'd been instructed to hand his passport, along with the money from Toronto, to Yannis Antonopoulos. This would get Yannis to Rome and back, as well as pay for various unspecified expenses. Then Yannis would return the passport. So I could hardly tell Nick to get lost—to send him packing back to his father—now could I?"

"Did *Michaelis* know Nick was involved?"

"Not at first."

"And Michaelis was actually in favour of this plan? This assassination?"

"It was his idea."

This astonished me. "You said it was Panagoulis' idea."

"They'd both arrived at the same conclusion. So they'd agreed to collaborate."

"And you were their channel of communication."

I expected her to smile, but she didn't.

"Michaelis finally saw things the way I did. Violence was the only way to get rid of the Colonels, otherwise they'd be around for ever, like Franco. But suddenly, *pouf*—they vanished. Abdicated, whatever. It was a miracle. The plan was off. Only by that time, Yannis had gotten himself arrested while carrying Nick's passport. The rest you know."

"Not quite."

Maria hesitated. I remained stubbornly silent, waiting for her to make up her mind.

Finally she said, "All right, Jim. He's staying with a family. Friends of mine, a couple and their two kids. Down the coast in Vouliagmeni."

A joyful warmth began to spread through my chest. I wanted to hug her, to shout something, but nothing emerged. I kept on waiting for more.

"We've had him there the whole time. Ever since he gave up his passport."

"Did it occur to any of you that Yannis might get caught? Carrying Nick's identity?"

"I know. I felt terrible about it the whole time. It was terribly risky for him. I kept wishing it were someone else—anyone but Nick—and yet he loved being part of something so important."

I believed her now. And yet, while in possession of the truth at last, I felt bitter. All those revolutionary heroics! And for what?

"Think of the *danger* you put him in, all of you," I burst out.

"Once Nick was in, he was in. It was his own choice."

"Couldn't you have talked him out of it—let somebody

159

else play the hero?"

"I doubt it. Anyway, it was Yannis who took the risks. Nick, on the other hand, has been perfectly safe, under protection, among friends, goes swimming every day at a private beach. *He's* tanned and healthy."

I'd broken out in a sweat. Under my clothes, my body was wet.

"I still don't see why Panagoulis needed Nick's passport. Couldn't he have bought one on the black market, like all the other terrorists?"

Maria shrugged. "As far as Alekos was concerned, it was a godsend: Nick had volunteered it. That made it far more precious than a passport that's been lost or stolen. The police aren't looking for it, it's perfectly valid, virtually above suspicion."

I tried another tack. "So if this was such a good plan, why was Yannis arrested at the airport?"

Now Maria looked upset. "Someone informed. I have my suspicions who, but I can't be sure."

"Then it's true Yannis was killed? That wasn't just a ruse of Costa's to scare me off?"

"God no." She looked stricken. There was a silence.

"Maria, how can they get away with this?"

"They're used to getting away with everything they do. Not having to answer to anyone."

So I'd been one of the last people to see Yannis alive — perhaps the very last who wasn't an executioner. Was there anything I could have done to prevent his death? I thought of the incipient terror I'd seen in his eyes, the mute appeal. He must have known who I was: why hadn't he asked me for help? Had he just been too self-disciplined? Too bent on martyrdom?

"Maria, I have to get to Nick now. Before anything else happens. Please give me the address in Vouliagmeni. Don't worry, I have a car. You don't need to be responsible for him any more."

"No."

"What?"

She returned my stare unapologetically. Suddenly, we

were right back where we'd started.

"Costa could be right, you know—the ESA could be watching you. So I couldn't give you the address even if I wanted to. I've told you too much already. We can't run the risk you'll lead them to Nick."

I tried to keep calm. "From what you've told me, he's done nothing particularly wrong. Apart from a foolish error in judgement, Nick is—"

"If you think that, you've learned *nothing* since you got here."

"I've learned to stop trusting you people. You all lie to me."

"All right. Listen. I'm not lying to you now. To imagine Drakonakis isn't looking for Nick would be like condemning him to death. Drakonakis is a *killer*, Jim—it's a documented fact. He gets permission directly from Ioannides to use torture. And remember, Ioannides is still free, still boss of the ESA. Nobody's had the balls to arrest him."

"But would they hurt a foreigner? A student? The international community would *crucify* Greece."

"You want to take that risk? What if the international community never found out? What if Nick simply disappeared without a trace and you couldn't prove anything?"

"Go on."

"Just stop: please. Stop trying to see him. He's been safe in Vouliagmeni for days now. And it's not just Nick—those people he's staying with are dear friends of mine, they put themselves at risk as a favour to me. For God's sake, don't endanger them too."

Maria reached across the table and pressed my hand. "I know this is hard on you, Jim. But it won't last much longer. In a few hours Nick will be out of here."

"Now what do you mean?"

"I've arranged passage for him on a ship. A freighter leaving tonight for Genoa." She could see how doubtful I looked, and added, "It's the best way, believe me."

"When is he leaving?"

"Around seven or eight. The captain's a great admirer of Michaelis, charter member of the party and all that. It's all set."

Somehow it sounded too good to be true, too easy. "But what about a new passport? Nick's going to need one in Italy, in case —"

"Forget it. There's probably a Canadian consulate in Genoa. Or Milan. He can get it replaced there. No big deal."

"I've already arranged one with the embassy here," I lied.

"He won't need it."

I toyed with a stainless-steel knife lying on the table, spinning it on its axis in one direction, then the other. "What's the ship called?"

"The *Tiresias*. Why?"

"I hope the captain doesn't mind another passenger. I'm a friend of the party too."

"Costa would have a fit."

"Maria, I'm sorry, I can't just take this on faith. Too many things haven't turned out the way they were supposed to. I have to see Nick with my own eyes. See him board that ship."

She sighed, giving a little shrug of futility. "Everything I do upsets Costa. I suppose this will be just one more thing."

"Is he jealous of you?"

"Jealous as hell."

"In love with you?"

"He's in love with Michaelis. Anyway, I'll have to check with the captain first." She seemed resigned to the idea of my going too. "But you'd better stay here in the meantime. Around six-thirty we'll drive to the pier."

"I can't do that." Some inner command directed me to reassert control. "All my things are at the hotel. And I haven't paid the bill. And besides, I have to pick up that new passport — Nick's going to need it, whatever you say. I don't want him getting sent back to Greece."

"Don't be absurd, that won't happen. Just pay the hotel by mail. And tell them to ship your things home. You can buy new clothes in Italy. Jim," she added, "you realize that nobody else would have gone to this trouble for Nick."

"I know."

She was silent.

"And I'm grateful, believe me." What more could I say? Yet I had to go against her. "Please don't worry. I understand

162

the dangers, I'll be ultra-careful. I promise I won't try to find Nick in Vouliagmeni."

As I stood up, alarm spread across Maria's face like a disfiguring stain: the look she'd had the night I told her I was going back to Una.

"Where are you going now? Listen, I levelled with *you*—"

I grabbed my jacket. "I know. I'll be at the pier before seven."

I ached with wanting her, but the old bond finally had to be cut. I got out of there just in time.

23

I t had cost me something to leave Maria. As I drove into the city, I thought I probably wouldn't know how much until later. And yet, entering the broad expanse of Vasillis Sophias, I could tell it had been the right decision. What Maria had said was true: I didn't really need to go to the embassy or the hotel, Nick's passport could be fixed up in Italy. But I'd been aware that there was still enough time before boarding the ship to fall "in love" with her yet again, and I simply couldn't afford that luxury, not now. There was too much at stake: not only Nick's safe passage, but my own existence as a separate being. I didn't want to cleave to Maria for ever.

If I'd stayed with her all afternoon, I'd have been ambushed by need as surely as that first night after leaving the shelter of the Trojan Horse, when she'd offered to lend me her Greek poetry collection, and I'd stepped inside her apartment "just for a minute", and three hours later my marriage — my life, as I then understood it — had begun collapsing, setting off the whole circuitous cycle of events that had put me into this rented car, which I was parking around the corner from the embassy in this vast folly of a city on my way to visit this other woman —

Helen, on the other hand, had been a benign presence: a helper, a guide. At the least, I could find out how she was handling her part in things, how she was dealing with Major Drakonakis, even with Mr. Ferrier. I felt I owed her something, too.

The clock hanging on the embassy wall said four-forty-five. This time the receptionist didn't try to make me wait among the stale newspapers but dialled straight through, and

Helen arrived immediately.

She didn't smile, just shook my hand correctly. Her glance was hurried, distracted. She looked changed from two days ago, different even from the revised mental image I'd been carrying around: paler, more serious and austere. There was a puffiness around her eyes. Her coral square-necked blouse revealed the delicate, fragile arc of her collarbone.

Once we were in her office and she'd shut the door behind us, the rigidity of her bearing fell away. "I'm so glad to see you," she said. "You never came in yesterday."

"I'm sorry. I've been awfully busy. Running around."

"Did the hotel give you my messages?"

"Actually I haven't been there since yesterday morning. What's wrong?"

"Drakonakis has put out a warrant for your son's arrest." Her eyes searched my face, as if looking for something she'd misplaced. "I don't understand," she said.

She's gone on her guard, I thought. Am I going to have to break with her, too?

"I can't explain," I told her. "I find that incredible." Which was true enough. "But Nick is alive—I know that much."

"Really? But that's wonderful!" She began looking happier. "How do you know?"

Helen's sincerity banished any doubts. I decided to trust her.

"Why does Drakonakis want to arrest Nick?" I asked.

"I don't know, that's what's so frustrating. It was John who spoke to him, but he's keeping it to himself. Something about Nick being a material witness—to what I'm not sure." After a pause she added, "John and I aren't getting along."

I thought I'd let that rest. "Helen, I'm going to tell you something I'd never tell anyone else. Nick is leaving Greece tonight, and I'm going with him. Only I don't want him going without papers. I'm worried about another screw-up with the authorities."

She listened without any change in expression. I went on, hoping this wouldn't turn out to be a blunder, but determined not to lose heart. "I'd like you to understand—Nick's done nothing wrong, he got mixed up with some people who talked him out of his passport, that's all. It's a long story, maybe I can explain it some day. But the ESA have killed one young man already and I have to get Nick away from here. Quickly."

She nodded soberly. "John doesn't think they—"

Virtually at the mention of his name, there was a peremptory knock at the door and Ferrier walked in without asking.

"Helen—" he began, then made a show of surprise at seeing me. "Oh, Mr. Urquhart—this *is* a piece of luck. We've been trying to locate you."

"So Helen's been saying. Can you explain what Drakonakis is up to?"

"We were hoping you could tell *us*."

"You've spoken to him. Surely he gave you some details."

"Not really. Said it came under the Official Secrets Act, or whatever they call it here. A matter of national security. Your son is wanted as a witness to attempted murder—that's all he'd say."

"Murder?" I didn't have to pretend to be shocked. "Whose murder?"

"'Attempted' is the operative word, I gather. On whom I don't know, but I got the impression it was someone very high up." Ferrier pursed his lips. "Mr. Urquhart, I can't help wondering: who *are* your son's friends?"

"I don't know all his friends. But I know who's been committing murder."

"I beg your pardon?"

"Drakonakis didn't tell you? The young man in his custody—the one you and I saw in that cell—is dead."

"Good God. Are you sure?"

"State torture isn't unknown in Greece. You're not exactly dealing with an honourable man."

"No. Still—" Ferrier drew himself up. "I'm afraid that doesn't change our position."

"Which is?"

"We've been asked by the Greek authorities to butt out. And we've agreed. It's in the hands of the Military Police now, a national-security matter. I'm afraid our hands are tied. Further meddling on our part would be a breach of diplomacy."

Ferrier's views were irrelevant, but I couldn't allow him to remain so smug, so damned comfortable with himself. "Is Ambassador Gordon home from the hospital?"

"Yes, sir. Why?"

"Please tell him something for me. I'll be calling on his assistance to find Nick—assistance you've failed to provide me. Tell him I'll be informing the minister in Ottawa, too. He'll want to know that."

Ferrier thought for a moment. Flustered but trying not to show it, he said, "Mr. Urquhart, if you don't mind, please come to my office before you leave the building, will you? It's just around the corner. First door on the right." He cast a glance of appeal, or warning, at Helen, before turning and leaving her office.

"I was too heavy," I told her.

"Not really. He asks for it. Please go on with what you were saying. Nick's papers?"

"Well, you've already done so much to help. But I have to ask for one more thing: can you give me a temporary passport for him? Something he can get home on?"

"You mean, without applying for it in person." Helen looked uncomfortable. I was asking her to go totally against her professional conditioning. "Well—there's a thirty-day replacement in case of loss or theft of a valid passport. But it has to be signed by the bearer, along with an application for renewal of the regular passport. And the signature has to be witnessed by an embassy official. Normally."

"Helen. This situation isn't normal."

"I know."

"To be honest, I'm afraid for Nick's life. That's what's at stake here."

She nodded.

"Will you do it? It doesn't have to be perfectly official—just something he can get by with. I know it's risky for you. You can imagine how risky it is for him."

"I'll make out an application in Nick's name. I can get all his data from the file. And I'll witness and authorize it.

But Nick will have to sign it himself, as soon as you give it to him. Okay? Please don't forget. The only problem is, the forms are locked in our safe, and the safe's in John's office."

"Christ."

"Don't worry, I'll think of a reason to go in there."

"What if he suspects what you're after?"

"He won't."

"Please tell him I didn't have time to see him. That I had an appointment or something. But Helen, I need that paper fast—the ship's leaving in a couple of hours."

"What time?"

"By seven."

"You leave the building now, and I'll wait half an hour —till five-thirty or so—and bring you the papers myself. Will you be at your hotel?"

"I'm going there now, but only long enough to get my things and check out. Then I'm going to Piraeus."

"Which pier?"

"Damn! I don't know." I was beginning to feel anxious. This was cutting it too close. "It's a freighter. The *Tiresias*."

"I'll find it. I'll be there by six-thirty at the latest."

"Helen, that's wonderful. You're fantastic."

I leaned across her desk and kissed her cheek. She smiled shyly, but didn't pull back. "See you at the dock," she said.

*   *   *

I walked out of the embassy feeling exhilarated. All that remained was to stop off at the hotel, get myself to Piraeus, and board that freighter with Nick.

Turning the corner, I saw a tall, casually dressed young man leaning against the front bumper of my Renault. Another guy sat inside, behind the wheel. Both of them had very short hair. Something told me they weren't car thieves, and there was no point in walking casually past, pretending it wasn't my car.

The one with his rear end on the bumper spoke before I could.

"Mr. Urquhart? I am Sergeant Stangos, Greek army. And this is Private Karanassopoulos. Do you mind to come with us?"

Just to reassure me, he added: "Please not to worry, please. We give you back your car later."

24

It was bad enough being hijacked by Drakonakis' men, not knowing if I'd ever get to the ship on time. Even worse was not knowing how they'd found me. Asking them directly would just raise their suspicions, so I could only speculate to myself as we drove the now-familiar route to ESA headquarters.

If they'd followed me all the way to the embassy, where had they located me in the first place? In Piraeus? At the Delfini? Had that been the meaning of Charalambos' warning glance as he left the hotel that morning? Or they might have seen me at Maria's. If they'd been watching her house, that meant they might still be watching *her*—and she'd unwittingly lead them straight to Nick at the ship.

An even grimmer possibility occurred to me: maybe the ESA had already found him. Maybe they were holding him for my arrival.... What an irony, Nick and I face to face at last, in Drakonakis' prison.

Sergeant Stangos took me directly to the major's office, knocking discreetly at the door, holding it open like a bellhop. Drakonakis was talking on the telephone. His brown military tie was askew, littered with cigarette ash, the jacket of his uniform flung across debris on his desk. He ignored our presence. When he'd finished talking, he swivelled around in his chair and nodded curtly to Sergeant Stangos, who backed out of the room, closing the door carefully behind him.

The major looked up at me with a certain repugnance. I was just a nuisance to him, another problem he didn't need. The feeling was mutual. I had to remind myself that I was the aggrieved, bereaved father—the victim of injustice.

I worked up my indignation.

"Major, what's going on here! Why am I picked up on the street like a common criminal?"

Drakonakis didn't stand. "Weren't my men nice to you? I told them to be." Reluctantly, I shook the large heavy hand he offered. "Coffee," he ordered.

"No thank you. How did you know where to find me?"

"Sheer luck. I was calling your friend Mr. Ferrier. He said you were there."

Drakonakis had no idea how much relief he'd just given me. Was that why Ferrier had tried to get me into his office? To delay my departure, so Drakonakis' men would have time to pick me up? Or had he been planning to warn me? How paranoid should I be? But it didn't matter now. Drakonakis had told me the one thing I needed to know — I hadn't been followed after all, either from Piraeus or from Kalamaki. Nick was safe. *And* Maria. Nick's departure was still on, even if mine wasn't.

Breathing more easily, I sat down without waiting to be invited. Drakonakis' broad forehead shone with sweat, his smooth countenance frayed at the edges. I could practically smell desperation rolling off him, along with the sour odour of his rough Greek cigarettes. How frantic he must be, I thought: having killed a prisoner, now he could be brought to justice for it, unlike the old days. He must be wild to cover his tracks, to invent some pretext or other to justify himself to the new order.

He said, "I wouldn't have picked you up if I didn't have some news for you."

"Good news?"

"Yes indeed."

"What is it?"

"Your son is alive and well."

"You're sure? Truly? That's incredible! How do you know? How did you find him?"

All at once the major lost his patience, releasing the anger he'd been hoarding so that I thought he might strike me. "You take me for a bloody fool? *Of course* I'm sure. And so are you, Mr. Urquhart. So let's stop playing games, shall we?"

"I beg your pardon?"

"I'm going to ask you some questions. I *insist* you answer them truthfully. If you don't, the consequences will be very serious. For you *and* your son."

I looked straight at him, the recommended defence when dealing with cops. "Major, I don't know what you're talking about. And I certainly don't like being threatened. I'm overjoyed you've located Nick—now will you please tell me where he is?"

He sighed wearily, wincing at a pain located somewhere inside of him. "I'll ask the questions. First: why did you visit Michaelis Kastri—not once, but twice in the past two days?"

"Why shouldn't I? Is it a crime to visit Michaelis Kastri?"

"He is an enemy of Greece. A Marxist, loyal only to Soviet Russia. He doesn't deserve to walk on Greek soil."

"I see."

"Before he was exiled, as you well know, he plotted with left-wing saboteurs to take over this country. Exile is too good for him."

"Michaelis isn't what you think," I said quietly. "He's no Marxist."

"Is that so? Then what is he?"

"A democratic socialist."

A bizarre sense of déjà-vu: once again I was pleading Michaelis' case, just as I had before the university board of governors—Michaelis, who was later to endanger my son's life, then keep him from me.

"Why are you so sure?" Drakonakis said.

"He and I worked together in Toronto. On a book." It was the simple truth. Yet saying it, in that setting, I felt practically accused out of my own mouth: the most innocent and innocuous facts became incriminating. "Actually," I said lamely, "Michaelis is intensely patriotic. He loves your country very much."

Drakonakis laughed humourlessly. "Of course. Kastri the great patriot." He burlesqued a polite interest: "So you work with him in Canada. Then you arrive here at the very same time he does, looking for your son—a strange coincidence, don't you think? Tell me, what are you and this

172

patriot planning for my country? Polite demonstrations? Civil disorder? Or just a straightforward *coup*, with the Russians invited for tea the next day?"

"I thought *coups* were more in your line."

"Next question: when is Alexander Panagoulis coming to join you?"

"I beg your pardon?"

"You are going to tell me he's a patriot too?"

Drakonakis' style of interrogation was making me nervous. I swallowed hard on a dry tongue and throat.

"I've heard of him, of course. Apart from that, I've no idea what you mean."

He leaned towards me, so close I could smell his rich blend of nicotine, aftershave, garlic, and rotting molars. He was enjoying this.

"Panagoulis," he said, the very name an incitement, "is not merely a criminal and an enemy of Greece, he's a goddamn lunatic. And a dangerous one. First, he attempts to dynamite the head of state. Then he resists arrest like a wild animal. He lies through his teeth to the court. He behaves in the most grossly abusive way to the judge and all the officers who have the unpleasant duty to guard him in prison."

"Were you one of them?"

"I was stationed in Patras at the time. But he abused the trust of many of my colleagues. He kept trying to escape, using every lying trick he could think of."

"I hear he succeeded."

"Only once! And then only because he seduced and bribed his way out. Of course he was recaptured. Panagoulis is an utterly worthless immoral man, Mr. Urquhart. And a *faggot*."

"I don't see what any of this has to do with my son," I said.

The major drew himself up into an assumption of dignity. "It has a great deal to do with him. I must know something—something that you, under Greek law, have an obligation to tell me. Kastri and Panagoulis have made an alliance. It's known only to their closest confidants, and to me. But I believe you are one of those confidants, Mr. Urquhart.

You are therefore in a position to tell me who are the others. In particular, you can identify the go-between — the link that Kastri and Panagoulis use for their communications."

I shook my head in mock dismay. "Major, even if what you say is true — which I doubt — how would I know anything about it? Do I look like a Greek revolutionary? I don't even —"

"Let's stop beating the bush. The prisoner upstairs, the one who claims he killed your son — you haven't even asked about him. You haven't asked what results our interrogation has produced. That proves your whole story is a hoax, because you already know the truth! Anyways, the prisoner has talked. He admits he is working for Panagoulis." Drakonakis paused for effect. I didn't contradict his use of the present tense. "He admits he is one of these young fools recruited for this so-called 'People's Army of Resistance'. How Panagoulis attracts them is beyond me. They're like him, I suppose — faggots with a persecution complex. They want martyrdom, I'll give it to them! Anyways, this Antonopoulos now says your son is his friend. That your son *gave* him the passport."

"Why would Nick do that? Give up his only proof of citizenship?"

"I wondered too. Then I found out you'd been visiting Kastri, and I put two and two together. Ah? Simple."

"Too simple, major. Don't confuse coincidence with fact. I'm a Canadian book publisher. And a father. And that's all."

He swept my words away with his hand. "I'll offer you a deal."

"I don't make deals with fascists."

He shrugged. "Very noble. But I am not a fascist. I am your one and only hope to get out of here — *with* your boy. Otherwise, both of you will be arrested as accessories to the crime."

"What crime?"

"That is none of your business."

"Major, if you're going to accuse me of crimes, I have a right to know what they are. Or are these just empty threats?"

I think he *would* have struck me then, had he thought he could get away with it; instead he just clenched his jaw and stared. It was almost more unnerving than a blow. My anxiety made a quantum leap.

"Okay," he said, "I'm going to ask you just two things. Two simple pieces of information. In exchange, you and your son may leave Greece without charges being laid. Without having to spend time in this prison."

"What two things?"

"One—where can we find him? Simply so we can go and question him. Oh, I understand he's been naïve, idealistic. Maybe even misled. We only need to ask him a few questions."

"What questions?"

"We'll see. Maybe you'll be allowed to be present. Two—again—who is the connection between Kastri and Panagoulis? I know they don't meet personally. They hate each other's guts, it's out of the question for them to talk face to face. I only need to know the third party's identity, Mr. Urquhart. That's all." He spread his hands wide, palms upwards, as if nothing could be more reasonable. "Tell me these small things, and you and your son are free men."

"May I think about it a minute?"

"Of course." The major looked satisfied, almost pleased. He turned his back to me and examined some papers on his desk, then jumped onto the telephone, speaking so rapidly I couldn't even make out the topic of his conversation.

Furiously, I tried to think, to consider all the angles. I asked myself if this could be the answer after all, the best hope for Nick: a far better guarantee of his safety than some risky, clandestine passage by freighter. But as much as I wanted his freedom, could it be worth purchasing at the price of Maria's safety? Even her life? Could I sacrifice her to my son one last time? For a moment I felt angry, confronted with such appalling choices. Then I remembered my own words—"I don't make deals with fascists"—and reminded myself what Drakonakis' promises were worth.

I waited until he was off the telephone.

"All right, major. I took my time because I needed a chance to understand you. I mean, it's all so incredible. The first time I came to see you, I came *voluntarily*, remember?

175

On the advice of my embassy. If I were really involved in this plot of yours, I'd hardly have come here at all, now would I? So my embassy knows all the facts of this case. They know about your prisoner—this Antonopoulos. And now I'm going to inform them of your threats. I'm going to ask them to lodge a protest with Prime Minister Karamanlis—no, hear me out—and with the Canadian government. Prime Minister Trudeau is very sympathetic to Michaelis Kastri, you know."

Drakonakis looked at me with all the expression of a lizard sunning itself on a rock. "Oh," he whispered. "Is that so?"

The silence that followed was more intimidating than any threats he might have uttered. It was his way of letting me know I'd gone too far.

By now, I'd given up all hope of ever joining Nick on board the ship. But I could still be useful to him. The longer I kept the major occupied, the likelier Nick would get away undetected.

"Major, I'd like to question Yannis Antonopoulos again. I suspect that's the best way to learn Nick's whereabouts. Why don't we talk to the prisoner together."

"Absolutely not."

"But why? Surely I have a right—"

"Right?"

"—to learn what's happened to my boy."

"Perhaps you're just interested in passing information to the prisoner."

"Another fantasy, major."

"The answer is no. Anyways, the prisoner is no longer here. He's been transferred to another jurisdiction."

"Is that heaven or hell?"

"I don't know what you're talking about."

"The prisoner is dead, isn't he?"

He gave an ugly, lopsided grin—a telltale admission. Then he cast his eyes heavenward and made a sucking sound with his tongue against his teeth, the Cretan way of saying no.

"Have I given you something to think about, major?"

"Absolutely. You've told me the lie Kastri is spreading about me. There's no place else you could have gotten that."

"If the story is true, what does the source matter?"

"Kastri is a source of nothing but lies."

"It wasn't Michaelis. Right now he's busy with far more important things than you."

"Like the overthrow of the state."

"The state seems to be changing, major. It may no longer have a place for people like you."

He stood suddenly, grimacing again, as if something had given way in his back. "It's time we ended this conversation. I regret you aren't prepared to be franker with me. Maybe you will be in a day or two."

"How could I be franker?"

"Think about it. Your son's freedom to leave Greece is at stake. He is now *officially* wanted for questioning on these counts—" Drakonakis rhymed them off on the fingers of his right hand "—theft of his passport, forgery of his passport, use of his passport in conspiracy to commit murder. And in general, the activities of the outlawed People's Army of Resistance. That will be enough to hold him in custody for a very long time. At least until the trial."

"Come off it, major. What conspiracy? What trial?"

He stood there looking down at me, his palms bracing the small of his back. "And it will be a criminal offence for you to refuse to co-operate—punishable by a prison term. I'm ordering you and your son to remain in Greece until this is cleared up. You will both require signed permission from me before you can leave the country."

"On whose authority?"

"My own. Don't worry: I have it."

I rose also, trying to think of further arguments to prolong our conversation.

"If I have anything to say about it, major, you're the one who'll be facing a murder charge."

He studied me a moment, trying to decide what to do.

"Go ahead," I taunted him. "Arrest me. If you try hard enough, you can find out everything I know."

But I couldn't goad him. His uniformed bulk was literally steering me out of the room.

"I'm informing my embassy about this," I said, backing towards the door. "It's an outrage."

"Go ahead. Do that." He pushed the door wide open onto the dismal corridor.

A soldier led me outside, another soldier brought my car around to the entrance. I drove away from the prison, a free man, technically.

25

I parked the Renault in a narrow back street on the fringe of the Plaka, just a few blocks from my hotel. The street seemed very quiet — construction work on a new office block had started, then been abandoned, apparently some time ago. For the moment I was unobserved; yet I had a disquieting sense my isolation wasn't going to last. Struggling to slow my steps and my anxiety, to appear unhurried just in case anyone was watching, I strolled as far as the cathedral before hailing a taxi. As I settled myself into the back seat, I felt sure no one had seen me.

By the time the taxi reached the docks in Piraeus, it was nearly seven-thirty. I could only hope the *Tiresias* hadn't departed on time. This was no time for Greeks to start being punctual.

Since I didn't know the number of the pier, we just had to keep driving along the street parallel to the docks until we saw a likely-looking freighter. My driver wanted to be helpful. He asked where the *Tiresias* was going, and I said Italy, and he pretended that meant he knew where it was berthed, unwilling to admit we were lost. He stopped and got out to question some bored stevedores hanging around waiting for their next job; a short, squat worker with a tanned skull waved us farther down the quay.

We carried on. I began to despair. Then I caught sight of Maria and Helen, standing close together beside a chain-link fence at the entrance to a pier. With their heads inclined towards each other, deep in conversation, they looked like two conspirators. Maria was silently intent, eyes fixed on the ground, while Helen explained something with a slow, sweeping gesture of her right hand, Helen holding her slender body self-consciously, as if she couldn't quite learn to coexist with the functional objects—loading cranes, winches, massive coils of grease-stained rope—surrounding her. Somehow I knew they were speaking Greek, not English. Abruptly I told the driver to stop.

Maria looked up and saw the taxi. As she and Helen turned to face me, I realized the mooring directly behind them was empty.

I concentrated on paying the driver. My bodily movements had suddenly grown heavy, resistant. With an effort I hoisted myself out of the cab and walked unsteadily past the two women, scarcely seeing them, to the far edge of the pier. Slowly, painfully, I raised my eyes to the horizon.

Maria walked up beside me and pointed towards the harbour mouth. Squinting into the low-lying sun, I followed the direction of her hand: a small, dingy tramp steamer, dwarfed by oil tankers and naval craft, was heading sluggishly out of port. Once painted white, the hull of the *Tiresias* was disfigured with streaks of rust. It still wasn't quite free of the harbour. It might as well have been a hundred miles out to sea.

I stared numbly at the shimmering outline of the ship. It gave an illusion of sitting stationary on the water, but if I took my eyes away from it a second, then looked back immediately afterwards, it had moved perceptibly closer to the horizon, ever so slightly, like a minute-hand creeping closer to the hour.

Maria and Helen were watching me. They seemed calm. For them, the story was over.

My gaze travelled from Helen's grey eyes to Maria's brown, then back out to the toy ship.

"Is Nick actually on board?"

"He wanted you to know he was sorry," Maria said.

"For what?"

"That he missed you. I couldn't get the captain to wait. We weren't even sure you'd make it."

"Neither was I."

"He's safe, Jim."

Helen said, "He has his papers now. He was so sweet, thanking me." She looked at me as if she could will my

180

unvoiced suspicions to rest. "I told him it was just part of my job."

"The ship arrives in Genoa Sunday," Maria said matter-of-factly. "He promised to phone Toronto from there. Let Una know he's all right."

She said nothing more. I felt my guard dropping as I let their assurances sink in.

From the set of Maria's mouth, I knew she was still angry that I'd left her in the afternoon, going against her will. But her judgement had been sound, and I thought she might as well know it; so I told her and Helen about being picked up outside the embassy and taken to ESA headquarters, about my interview with Drakonakis, his threats.

Maria's eyes narrowed, darting a look of concern at Helen. The bond of complicity between them seemed to crack.

Helen picked this up at once. "I guess I should go now."

"No," I said, "it's all right. Isn't it, Maria?"

Maria paused, looking from me to Helen. "Yes," she said grudgingly, "it's all right."

"I didn't tell him anything," I said. "Except that I know Yannis is dead."

"But that's plenty. It tells him Michaelis knows."

"Is that really so bad?"

She paused to think. "Maybe not. Maybe they'll be more cautious now. We've got to use the information before they do any more harm. Michaelis has to convince Karamanlis the ESA is out of control."

And all I could think was that, at last, Nick would be clear of it all.

I looked for the ship again. This time it took me a moment to locate it on the horizon, beyond the other shipping. I pictured Nick out on deck, maybe talking to a crew member—or was he standing at the railing, watching the shore, looking at me but not seeing me, as I was not seeing him?

We were all silent for a moment. Finally Maria broke in, a low note of urgency entering her voice: "You can't stay here, you know."

I could see she wouldn't be denied this time.

"You're right. I'd better go straight to the airport."

"No, no. The ESA has men there. Drakonakis may have given them your description." She hesitated. "You know Crete, don't you?"

She knew I did. Long ago I'd told her about Una and me travelling there—ironic, since Maria's mother had been Cretan, and as a girl Maria had spent the summers at her grandparents' home on the south coast; she'd once told me she'd been staying there, age eighteen, at the very moment Una and I were on the north coast.

"What about it?"

Maria was searching her shoulder-bag for something. "The ferry for Iraklion leaves at eight. If you hurry, you'll just make it." She found what she'd been looking for and pressed it into my palm: an old-fashioned, oversized key, quite rusted and heavy, attached to a black beadwork key-chain in the shape of a cross. "This opens my house in Eleftheria. You can't miss it—the only house built out over the water. Just ask for *'to spiti tis Kyrias Marias'*. The people will know which one."

"But why?"

"The ESA won't be paying attention to the ferries. You can fly from Crete direct to London. Or if you're not in a rush to get home, a few days in Eleftheria might do you good. It's very isolated. Anyway, let's get you out of here. You have to go somewhere."

*   *   *

The next half-hour passed in a blur—a haze of sweet relief and deep regret. Suddenly I seemed unable to make decisions, to take charge. My control had shaken loose. I knew at last where Nick was. Where was I?

I was standing at the railing of a large white car-ferry about to depart for Crete. Helen had left to find a taxi that would take her back to her real life. Only Maria remained, lingering on the quay below me, as if she had nowhere else to go, nothing else to do but see me off.

182

I looked down into her upturned face. We stared at each other, oblivious of everything else. She looked so small, miniature, down there. A shudder seemed to go through her as the ship's whistle let out a blast. The ropes were being cast off, the water churning at the stern as the ship backed delicately away from the pier. For a moment I felt an agonizing surge of the old desire—wanting her, as I looked down into her offered eyes, as much as I could remember wanting anyone. A part of me would have given anything to have Maria back again, like someone prepared to throw everything away for one last drink. Yet I was powerless to act on the desire. To make the world spin in the opposite direction. The process of departure had gone too far.

As the big ship manoeuvred itself into its lane, starting for the open sea, I leaned over the railing to return her wave. For the last time I asked myself why we hadn't seized our moment, our opportunity to be together after all, to do things right for once. But of course there had been no such opportunity: no so-called right moment, with the so-called right person. Maria wasn't going to return to Canada, not after everything that had happened, any more than I was going to abandon home and work and colleagues to start all over in Greece. Both of us knew that. It was as out of the question as beginning anew with Una. But there *was* something wonderful about the dumb loyalty we felt for each other, the compulsion that refused to die completely, the hopeless yearning for the impossible, unreachable, ever-retreating love—eternally *in absentia*. Surrounded by the magnificent ugliness of Piraeus harbour, I set out for Crete as I had twenty-one years before, only this time I sailed alone.

26

The ferry docked at Iraklion a little after six the next morning, opposite two navy gunboats. I filed along the deck and down the gangway among soberly dressed Cretans and tanned long-haired kids shouldering packs, rubbing sleep from their eyes—Nick's contemporaries. I was travelling lighter than any of them: no luggage, nor any ticket or reservation. No one was expecting me. Freedom indeed! My only burden was Maria's key, made of iron from the heft of it, weighing down the side pocket of my suit jacket. I still hadn't decided whether to gain access to Maria's house on the south coast, or simply go straight to the airport and book myself on the first flight to London.

Immediately I liked feeling the island's toughness under my feet again. Leaving the young travellers to fend off hotel touts and taxi drivers who'd come down to meet the ferry, I set off for the town on foot.

I passed the little Venetian fortress, its square walls keeping watch over the few fishing boats that hadn't already gone out before dawn. Yellow nets and waterstained wicker baskets lay heaped on the decks, unprotected from thieves; robbing a fisherman's livelihood, even on infamously thieving Crete, was unthinkable. Then the Twenty-Fifth of August Street, slanting upwards into the heart of town. I followed it with excited expectation—strange, considering I had no idea where I was going, or what I was looking for.

The shops weren't open yet. I was struck by the sheer number of them catering to tourists, far more than I recalled from the fifties—car-rental agencies with multilingual signs, photography shops, pharmacies, banks, places advertising "Cretan Art", their windows displaying island embroideries and white sheepskin rugs alongside a hodgepodge of souvenir ashtrays and chintzy "antiques" and poor copies of classical vases. Farther along, in cluttered Venizelou Square, people and automobiles passed me on their way to work.

Despite the advent of tourism, there was still a neglected feel about the place: Iraklion hadn't lost its shiftless indifference, its resemblance to a thieves' market. The Venetian fountain, a giant stone wash-basin for the seventeenth-century lions prowling around its base, still stood in the centre of the square, ignored by everyone.

I selected a *kafenion* at random from several opening onto the square. I took a table in a shaft of warm dusty sunlight, just inside the open windows, where I could observe the teeming life outside. Almost certainly Una and I had sat there once. Yet to the people passing by, I had no connection whatever to them or their town — I was just another intruder passing through, as alien as the Venetian lions.

After a cheese pie and a good deal of sludgy Greek coffee, I retraced my steps down the Twenty-Fifth of August Street to a little establishment I'd passed on my way up. It had been closed then, but now was open for business. "Byron Rent-a-Car", the awning said.

A plump, nearsighted young man with a scarcely perceptible limp told me I was his first customer in two days. Steam from his coffee cup rose past a detailed map of Crete on the wall and an Olympic Airways calendar illustrating the sanctuary at Delphi. As he filled out the forms, squinting at my driver's licence through his bifocals, he complained about the German and Swedish governments sending 727s to the island to remove their nationals, the tour operators cancelling all their bookings. Even the resort hotels were talking about closing before the season ended, he said, and before they got commandeered for military purposes, like the hotels on Cyprus.

"The only ones coming are the heepies. And they don't have any money."

Luckily for Byron Rent-a-Car, some of us weren't prudent enough to do the sensible thing. I checked the wall map: the road to Eleftheria would take me straight through Ayios Nikolaos.

Beyond the ragged eastern suburbs, the road ran past the airport, then parallel to a new superhighway built under the junta. I stayed on the old road. The landscape fit into the contours it had carved in my brain two decades earlier: I kept experiencing sharp bursts of recognition, making an S-turn between sheer faces of bleached rock, honking to warn invisible drivers I was coming, passing a banana plantation on my right, the immense, turquoise sea scrolling in on my left. The sheep and goats grazing in the yellow grass along the shore would be descendants of the same ones we used to see back then.

Eventually the road climbed into bald foothills, dry and dotted with silvery olive trees and dusky green carobs growing in footholds of reddish soil among the rocks. The light became dazzling as the road climbed higher. Finally I was in the mountains. Negotiating a series of passes with steep drops on either side, I skirted the town of Neapolis, descending again towards sea-level, winding at last tortuously down, into Ayios Nikolaos.

Saint Nicholas in English, plain Ayios to temporary residents such as Una and me: I'd never expected to see it again. I arrived at the U-shaped port, crossed the small bridge that separated the harbour from the so-called bottomless lake. According to legend, the lake was connected by undersea passage to Santorini in the north. But as ever, it was performing its real-life function as a shelter for fishermen to tie up their caiques and sit and drink and gossip outside their favourite café under the pepper trees. I pulled up by the café and let the engine idle. Tourist shops and restaurants had sprung up around the port, sporting bright yellow canvas awnings and blue-and-white umbrellas. No sign of the rusty packet steamer that used to visit twice a week on its way to and from Rhodes—or of the Rififi, the restaurant where Una and I had taken our evening meals. The Rififi had been torn down, and was in the process of being replaced by a more ambitious structure.

I drove around the west side of the port onto the Ammoudi road. Facing the rocky shore where Una and I had liked to stroll because it was private, hidden from the town by a bend in the road, were two new, large white hotels. They were a startling sight, their luxury and modernity incongruous in that setting. They flew British, German, French, Swedish, and American flags beside the Greek one, above their entrances facing the sea. Decals on the glass doors advertised "Hellascars" and "Barclaycard" and "Diners Club" and "Exchange/Change/Wechsel", but nobody was around needing currency exchanged. A man dressed as a waiter slumped alone in the shade of an umbrella, staring off into space.

I turned back into town, parked the car by the white-washed curb of the main street, and walked up the east side of the harbour, the side I'd avoided until now. Just past the Lato Hotel, between low buildings with orange tile roofs, an archway spanned a broad flight of public steps. I climbed the steps to a stony path at the top. The path wound among the few white houses perched on that hill, a neighbourhood called Milos. I passed a garden of scarred cacti, lost my bearings, circled back, and finally found a particular dirt track baked iron-hard by the sun. Sternly I marched myself along it.

The whitewashed stone house was still there. Even smaller than I remembered, it had a prospect even more magnificent: directly across the huge, dark blue Gulf of Mirabellou to the massive mountains on the far eastern shore. Una and I had seen those mountains every morning on waking in our narrow bed. I could still visualize how their appearance changed as the day wore on: a misty silhouette when the sun rose behind them, this silver austerity at noon, then a late-afternoon clarity when the declining sun bathed the peaks in light from the west, picking out details on the lower slopes — trees, villages, roads — with photographic precision. And after dark, the lights of distant villages and automobiles would shimmer and signal towards the little house, to whoever lived here now.

The house had a small garden and an equally small concrete terrace, shaded by a grapevine overhead. The doors and shutters were washed a sun-faded turquoise. A work shirt was draped over a chair, and snapdragons and geraniums flourished in old olive-oil cans; the place was occupied, presumably by locals. Like Maria's house in Kalamaki, it had the curious characteristic of two doors, even though the house contained only two rooms. The door on the right led into the bedroom where Nick had been conceived.

I couldn't look at the place without feeling overwhelmed. I took a last, quick, blurred glance: what a short time had passed since Una and I had lived there, a blink of history's eye, yet in the meantime whole worlds had collapsed, or been casually, thoughtlessly torn up by the roots. I wished Nick could have come with me to see this simple place where his existence had begun, but knew I'd be the only one to bear witness.

*   *   *

Continuing east along the old road, I left the coast and took the right-hand turnoff to Ierapetra. It was the route Minoan traders had followed to the south coast, to what's now called the Libyan Sea. Even though I drove slowly, it took scarcely half an hour to cross the island and reach the other side.

A crude, simple, forgotten place, Ierapetra: flat-roofed and low to the ground, resembling some Arab outpost on the edge of the desert. For all practical purposes, this was where Europe ended. Ierapetra had been the last town on Crete to fall to the Romans, who probably wondered why they'd bothered. So far, tourism seemed to have bypassed the town completely.

I stopped for a *gasosa* at a small café facing the waterfront, a flat curving expanse of sand, home to a couple of dozen caiques. Beyond, the featureless sea stretched indifferently to a horizon wan with heat.

I was the café's only customer. A boy in a threadbare white shirt served my drink, ignoring a large elderly pelican standing beside the café entrance. Perhaps the pelican was a sort of mascot. Its jutting bill and rheumy eyes gave it an air of aloof misanthropy. It was also unwell, to judge from the slimy green deposit trailing between its webbed feet.

The drink didn't revive me as I'd hoped it would. It may have been the heat getting to me, or the knowledge that the last stage of my journey lay ahead, waiting for me. I'd enjoyed the sense of movement, of passage, and was reluctant to have it end. I'd been stringing things out, stopping first in Iraklion, then Ayios Nikolaos, now here, not wanting to stay anywhere too long. After Eleftheria, there would be nowhere else to go. I wasn't sure I even wanted to see Maria's house. Yet if I went back to Ayios, I'd get swallowed by the past, and if I stayed here, in the dead atmosphere of Ierapetra, something told me I'd wind up sick and misplaced as the pelican.

The sun, reflecting off water and rock, was behind me as I drove, affording a fine sight of the primaeval coastline up ahead. After some tomato fields sheltered on the seaward side by reed fences, there were few signs of human habitation apart from the road, which was narrow but reasonably well built; it wound up and around steep rocky slopes fringed with crouching trees, switching constantly back on itself, blind turns masked by sheer cliffs. Every so often the road suddenly burst out above a precipice that dropped straight down to water so magnificently turquoise I was tempted to stare and stare, instead of concentrating on oncoming vehicles. Yet there was hardly any traffic. As the crow flew, the distance to Eleftheria wasn't great, but it seemed to go on for ever. The process of constantly turning the wheel one way, then back hard the other, was hypnotic.

A tiny hamlet emerged from nowhere. Not even signposted, it passed so quickly it might have been imagined.

A few kilometres farther along, down at sea level, I came to another village, a handful of stunted buildings announced by a road sign thick with dust. *Eleftheria*. I was there.

27

E leftheria was a huddle of stone houses and animal sheds constructed all of a piece, bisected by a single unpaved street — a place for gnomes or recluses. Rather than block the narrow street, I left the car beside the road at the entrance to the village and entered on foot, my jacket slung over my shoulder. Low wooden doors, eaten by insects and time, barred the heat from tiny homes whose interiors I could only imagine. I was wondering if anyone still lived there when I turned a corner and came upon a tiny grocery store with an ancient woman in front of it.

She was sitting by her open door, wearing a white kerchief. Her long white apron covered a black dress that made no concessions to the heat, yet she was sunning herself there, like an old cat hoarding the light before it deserted her life. A hand-fashioned cane rested in her lap. Outwardly, her place looked indistinguishable from the other houses. Only a few detergent boxes and tinned goods dimly visible on the shelves behind her identified it as a shop, no doubt the only one in the village.

The old woman was almost toothless. Her waxy flesh had receded gracefully around the contours of her skull; her eye sockets were set deep into her head, yet the eyes themselves flashed a knowing and amused curiosity. If my arrival surprised her at all, she certainly didn't let on.

I wished her good day and asked where I could find *to spiti tis Kyrias Marias*. She nodded slowly. This was what she'd expected me to say: the only reason foreigners ever came to Eleftheria.

In a voice hoarse with age but still remarkably powerful, she instructed me to follow the street until the end, then turn right. Maria's *mother's* house was the big one, she said, the one outside the village. But nobody was home. Maria's mother was dead now. And Maria herself was away — far away — in the capital! She uttered the word proudly, as though it were an extraordinary achievement to have reached Athens.

I told her I understood: I'd been with Maria in Athens. Fishing the key out of my jacket, I displayed it to show her I was going inside.

Her eyes narrowed. With some difficulty she leaned forward, gingerly touching the black beadwork cross with fingertips as white as ivory. She raised the wrinkled folds of her eyes to mine. It was old, she said, Maria's *mother's mother's* key.

Evidently the old woman had known Maria's grand-mother. Perhaps they'd been friends? I thanked her, wished her good day once more, and continued down the street, which quickly deteriorated into a track strewn with sheep droppings. I encountered no one else. A couple of derelict caiques were pulled up onto the sand where the street finally petered out entirely as it merged with the shoreline. I'd been mistaken to think of Ierapetra as the end of things. This was.

As Maria had said, I couldn't miss the house. It stood aloof from the village, built on a rocky promontory right out over the water. In scale and design, it was utterly unlike anything else in Eleftheria. There were two storeys, the upper more ample than the lower, jutting out over the water's edge and supported by four square whitewashed pillars resting on the outcropping of rock. The pillars supported a weathered wooden balcony that wrapped itself around the house, open to the sea and sky; once painted blue, the balcony had flaked and faded from long exposure to the elements, like a sky clouded over.

The main door was at the side of the house. I approached it by a path laid with large flat stones. Beyond the door, the seaward wall was accessible only by climbing over massive boulders, a stout barrier against pounding waves — not a necessity at the moment, however, since the sea was placid. The house faced a cove with an unobstructed view all the way to invisible Africa.

Maria's family had been the village gentry. If the old woman at the grocery had known Maria's grandmother, I realized, it would have been as a servant, not a friend. I inserted Grandmother's key into the lock and turned it, encountering resistance. The mechanism was so stiff I had to use all my strength before it gave way, jarringly and reluctantly, with a heavy *clunk*, showering rust particles onto my wrist. The door swung inwards of its own weight, as if someone had pulled it open from inside.

The dark interior was surprisingly cool and moist. All the windows had been tightly shuttered, both inside and out, preserving a thick musty smell, an accumulation of undisturbed dampness. The only source of light was the open doorway behind me, so I left the door ajar. As my eyes adjusted, I made out heavy black beams in the ceiling, a central room with an enormous fireplace, a staircase with a railing, and, off to the right, a large and primitive kitchen.

Automatically I gravitated to the kitchen: long rectangular wooden table, counter inlaid with old white tiles glazed with a heraldic blue pattern. Blackened pots and frying pans hung from hooks above an iron woodstove. The stove had been superseded by a two-burner hotplate resting on top of it. A butane canister was attached to the hotplate by a rubber hose, and a faint suspicion of stale gas hung in the air. I wondered how long it had been since Maria had come here.

Back in the main room, I came across fragmentary relics of her visits. A dogeared *Observer* colour magazine dating from March 1967, just before the Colonels seized power: memento of happier times. A huge ragged poster of Che Guevara in his heroic pose, one corner peeling off the wall. A sleeve for The Doors' *Waiting for the Sun* album, no record inside. I looked around for a record player but couldn't locate one. On the dusty bookshelves made of bricks and boards, old Penguin paperbacks were lined up in their orange and green uniforms.

I could picture Maria's summer vacations here, a dark-eyed child, before she'd gone to Cambridge or emigrated to Canada or even suspected the existence of anyone like me. She'd been doted on, spoiled by her parents and grandparents, she'd been given the freedom to swim off the rocks, to roam the countryside at will, granddaughter of the village notables. Yet her family's standing hadn't prevented an incident she'd related to me once (with remarkable acceptance, I'd thought), about a shepherd accosting her in the hills behind the town when she was seven or eight; he'd grabbed her, firmly but unviolently, and held her close, rubbing himself against her repeatedly before releasing her.

The grandparents had died when Maria was a teenager, followed a few years later by her father. After that, she'd had the place pretty much to herself. Her mother preferred to stay home in Athens, so Maria had come here on her own, sometimes inviting friends or lovers from the city. No doubt they'd been directed to the house by the old woman at the grocery.

Craving light and air, I climbed the stairs. They were made of terracotta tiles set into worm-eaten wooden risers, the handrail rubbed smooth by the palms of Maria's ancestors. Lord knows how many generations back the house went —certainly to the Turkish occupation. At the top, a bolted door. It brought me out onto the gallery that ran across the face of the house.

It was a wonderful sensation—like walking into the sky. The blue air was lovely and warm. No longer searing hot, the sun hung lower now, already close to the hazy mountaintops in the west where I'd come from. The sea washed gently against the rocks below the balcony. I sat down on the weathered grey planks with my back against the wall, took off my shoes and socks, and extended my feet out over the water.

* * *

I remained there so long I lost track of time, just allowing the sense of peace to seep into me. Gentle eddies of air caressed and cooled my mind.

At last I felt a kind of gratitude about the journey I'd made: not only because Nick was safe, and because I'd done what I could for him, but because Maria and I had finally left each other properly, with love.

193

I watched the sky turn a deep crystalline blue. It seemed suspended above the dark sea by a couple of ice-blue stars. No moon. No sound, apart from the steady sloshing of the waves, the cries of children off in the village. On the cooling air, the smell of wood smoke and olive oil. Apparently life was going on in Eleftheria, if nowhere else. Civilization was continuing in some form. What more could a human being ask?

*   *   *

I heard the noise faintly at first. It seemed to be coming from somewhere inside the house. Not especially alarmed, but remembering I'd left the front door open, I went back inside and paused at the top of the staircase to listen. I heard the scraping of wooden chair legs being dragged across the tile floor downstairs, followed by a loud thud—as if a large and clumsy creature were barging into things.

The sounds weren't furtive in the least: the smack of a metal utensil on the kitchen counter, the clink of a glass against a plate, the sluggish cough of the tap followed by a splattering of water into the sink. Whoever was down there was making no attempt to hide it. Presumably, then, it was someone who knew the place. Surely there could be no thieves in such a village. I proceeded softly downstairs.

By now the interior was in total darkness. The electricity, if any, must have been shut off. Feeling for each step with a stockinged foot, I paused at the foot of the staircase. I didn't want to startle the person.

A soft, golden glow emanated from the kitchen. I could see a huge shadow projected against one wall, looming and shrinking as the intruder moved about. Or was I the intruder?

I moved slowly across the dark central room. The front door, I noticed, had been closed. I was about to call "Hello?" when my digital watch beeped the hour. The unseen presence in the kitchen reacted instantly—an abrupt cessation of movement, a frozen silence, waiting, while I did the same.

I heard a soft outlet of breath. In a moment a silhouetted

figure appeared in the kitchen doorway, blocking out the light, holding a butcher knife. Although the face was completely in shadow, I knew the body's elongated, awkward stance so well that I just said, "I don't think you'll be needing that."

"When are you going to stop following me around?" Nick asked conversationally.

28

He threw the knife behind him, a blind careless motion. It landed with a noisy clatter on the table beside a burning kerosene lamp. We approached each other warily—two divers encountering each other in the depths, unexpectedly coming upon the same reef from different directions. I raised and spread my arms. Nick hesitated, then floated into my embrace.

I hugged the long hard spareness of his back. It was so wonderful, so incredibly right, just to feel the solid reality of him pressed up against my chest. I could only keep wordlessly squeezing his upper arms, his angular bony shoulders, a spicy, primitive smell rolling up from both of us. I could have wept.

At first Nick hung there, suspended by the pressure of my arms. Finally he gave me a short, sharp hug in reply.

Breaking apart wordlessly, we stared into each other's eyes for the briefest of moments. Immediately he turned away, stumbling back into the kitchen. We took chairs on opposite sides of the table. He pulled the lantern between us; I pushed it down the table, so the glare wouldn't hide his face. We hunched towards each other, our bare forearms almost touching, his browner and more sinewy than mine.

I said, "I thought you'd be halfway to Italy by now!"

"Me too." He was grinning tightly, shaking his head in disbelief. "And I thought you'd be halfway *home.*"

There *was* something different about him: I felt I was looking into the face of a new Nick—a familiar stranger, a half-son. What was it? Even under the couple of days' growth of beard, his cheeks were visibly thinner, more concave. He'd let his hair grow. It swirled about his tanned forehead, framing it in curls bleached by the sun. His dark hornrims gave him an owlish air, completely at odds with the wildness of his hair and the glinting blond stubble on his tanned chin. And although he'd aged a little during our time apart, paradoxically he also seemed freer, looser in his limbs.

The other difference was in the way he spoke. Through some sea-change I could only guess at, Nick had acquired an accent, indeterminate in origin — not quite English, not quite Greek, yet definitely no longer North American. His speech now had a precise, considered inflection, making even quite ordinary words seem chosen for their exactness. It was the accent I'd heard on Costa's tape.

"Why," he said, "did you come *here*?"

"I was about to ask you the same thing."

Neither of us wanted to be the one who revealed the mystery, ended the game — we couldn't bear to expose ourselves in each other's presence.

Finally I had to break the silence. "It was Maria's idea. She gave me a key. I was going to take it easy for a couple of days."

He grinned at me. "She gave me one too. I sure wasn't expecting the door to be open."

The grin vanished, and through his glasses he looked at me with guarded curiosity, reserving judgement.

"You hungry?" he said. "I was just about to eat." He nodded toward a battered khaki backpack sitting on another chair. I hadn't noticed it before; a grimy Canadian flag patch had been sewn onto the flap. He rummaged inside it: "Some humble fare I picked up in Ayios Nikolaos.... Isn't that where you and Mum stayed once?"

Wondering what had happened to the soft-sided Samsonite bag I'd bought him as a going-away present, I realized the pack must contain all his travelling gear. From somewhere inside it he retrieved a length of thick sausage and half a circular loaf of bread. Reaching behind him, he pulled a chipped plate off the counter and dropped the sausage and bread onto the plate, hacking off thick slices with the knife. I watched these movements with dumb fascination. Then he reached into the pack again and drew out a small bottle of

197

the local retsina, which he placed ceremoniously between us.

"Sorry it's not a classier wine. All I could afford."

"I'm trying to cut down on my drinking."

"Really?" He shrugged. It was no concern of his. "Retsina's probably safer than water here. Anyway. Help yourself."

He spoke as the host. I was the guest, the interloper, after all. But I was touched by his offer of hospitality, and hungry besides. I popped a slice of the gristly, garlicky sausage into my mouth.

"So how did you get here?" It was just one of a thousand questions I wanted to ask him.

Chewing hard, he paused to think a moment, then said, "Hitched rides, mostly. Got picked up by a truck full of these gas things." He nodded his head towards the butane canister behind him. "Caught the bus from Ayios Nikolaos to Ierapetra and hitched from there. I thought it would take a lot longer. Everybody's quite willing to pick you up."

"Yes, but I mean—why aren't you on the ship?"

Pausing in the process of dismantling bread with his fingers, Nick looked up at me innocently. "Didn't they tell you it was docking in Iraklion?"

"You were going to stay on board. Weren't you? All the way to Italy. Wasn't that the plan?"

"Yeah. So?"

"So, it isn't safe for you to be in Greece."

He grinned knowingly, as if I were a bit of a simpleton but harmless enough, deserving of his indulgence. Once again he dove into his pack—it seemed to hold the answer to everything—and this time extracted a crumpled newspaper. From the front page, I recognized it as one of the leftwing Athens dailies. He held it open, displaying a banner headline above a photograph of Michaelis in full cry, orating behind a battery of microphones.

"Can you translate?" I asked.

"More or less: 'Kastri Accuses ESA of Murder. Athens Man Died in Custody. Government Decommissions Officer while Case Investigated.' Like that."

"Drakonakis?"

Nick nodded vehemently. Using the knife, he jimmied

the cap off the retsina bottle. "Do you mind?" He took a long swallow straight from the neck, not bothering with a glass. "My ship put in at Iraklion at noon. I came ashore for a quick look round, only expecting to stay a few minutes, then I saw this newspaper and realized I don't have to run any more. I have nothing to worry about. I'm going to testify against the bastard."

"Testify?"

For a second, his mouth quivered. He immediately returned the bottle to his lips.

"*Yasu*," he said, belching softly.

"*Yassas*." My stomach was growing tighter. "Nick, if I were you, I wouldn't get involved in that trial. I wouldn't even count on there being one."

"No? Why not? Anyway," he added quickly, "you're *not* me."

The flare of his banked anger was like a glimpse of heat lightning in the distance: a split second, and it was gone.

"There's no telling how this thing will turn out," I continued quickly, "it could backfire on Michaelis. The court could quite easily decide in the ESA's favour, you know, you can't count on justice here."

"I *know* that."

"Well? Wouldn't it be a lot smarter to stay out of it?"

"Are you going to start telling me what to do and think?" he said softly.

"I'm just being realistic. After what you've been through.... I mean, haven't you had enough?"

"Christ! Enough of what? How do you know what I've been through? Do you realize you nearly got me arrested in Athens? Not to mention endangering my friends — people I care a lot about. Why not just go home and leave me alone?"

I felt an impulse to reach out: whether to embrace or slap him, I couldn't tell. "Would you prefer I didn't give a damn what happens to you?"

"That might be an improvement."

I was so taken aback, so stung by this, I said nothing.

"Listen," he said. "If it weren't for your 'help', I'd still be back there."

"Sure you would. In an ESA prison. We had to get you away. Everybody thought so: Costa, Maria—"

"They only thought that because of you."

"You sound pretty angry."

"Spare me the psychology shit, okay?"

This was the biggest change of all—this blunt, undisguised anger, from the heart. Nick had always acted circumspectly with me before, self-contained.

I decided to back off a little. I said nothing, just watched his face, illuminated by the unearthly glow from the lantern as if by an interrogator's lamp. He tipped his chair and body backwards into the shadows, trying to melt into them, to vanish from my sight.

"So what else does it say in the paper?"

He sat forward again. "It's pretty straightforward. Michaelis blew the whistle on the ESA. Even the right-wing press printed the story. It's too sensational to ignore."

"Did he name Drakonakis?"

"Not yet—just 'ESA thugs', 'military servants of the fascist clique'. Stuff like that."

"Does the story identify Yannis?"

"Oh yes—" He stopped himself.

"You?"

"Of course not. Why should it?"

"You were involved with him, weren't you?"

He shrugged. "So were a lot of people. Way more than me. And they aren't mentioned."

"Panagoulis?"

"No."

"Or Costa? Maria?"

He stared at me in mock innocence. When I refused to look away, his eyes moved off, then returned slowly to mine. "How much do you know about all this?"

I wanted to be able to trust him. "I'm not sure."

"What did Yannis say when you saw him in prison?"

"That you were dead. Imagine how I felt when I heard *that.*"

Nick shook his head, giving a weird, sad, private smile. He looked across to a dark corner of the kitchen, to something only he could see. "Yeah, I heard. That was his line. He wanted to protect me—throw the bastards off my track." Slowly he toppled forward onto the table, burying his face in his arms, so that I could see only the top of his head.

I waited for a moment, then said: "When I saw him, he looked terrified."

Nick lifted his head suddenly and looked at me. "He was right to be, wasn't he? He knew damn well what they'd do to him. And he never gave me away—Jesus!" He sniffed loudly. "Yannis knew he was going to die, they all knew. And they accepted it. He had to be the martyr."

"Oh Nick," I said. "Why did you get involved with him? With all those people and their craziness?"

He sniffed again. "They're not crazy. They're good people."

"Idealists."

"Exactly."

"Like you."

"Far more than me. Compared to them, I'm just a dilettante along for the ride." He blew his nose into a handkerchief that hadn't seen soap and water for weeks. "And then there's Maria. You think she's crazy? She made sure I was looked after. Small world, eh?" He stared fixedly at me, daring me to read his eyes.

"You met her once. Remember? In my apartment."

"Yeah. I almost didn't recognize her." Emotion thickened his voice—an echo, I assumed, of his feeling for Yannis.

"Go on about Yannis and you."

He sighed. "I didn't really know him that well. We only met once, just before he left Athens for Rome. But I liked him. We were going to celebrate after he returned my passport."

"Celebrate what?"

"Did they tell you his assignment? From Panagoulis?"

"Another dynamite attempt?"

He seemed relieved that I knew, and that I wasn't acting outraged. "No—Panagoulis was haunted by the failure of that one. This time it was supposed to be a clean kill. With a rifle."

"Could Yannis shoot?"

"Fantastic marksman, apparently. He learned during his military service."

Somehow this didn't sound like sufficient preparation for the job. "Nick, think a minute: imagine if he'd been captured. He'd have been carrying *your* passport. You'd have been linked to the assassination of a head of state!"

Unexpectedly, with something like happiness, he grinned. "I know."

"What," I almost yelled, "would have been the point?"

"Greece."

I just stared.

"Well, *you* love Greece." He said it in complete earnestness, prompting me. "At least you always said you did. If anybody understands this, it should be you."

"Only—"

"So isn't it worth risking something for?"

"But your life? This wasn't *your* battle, Nick. Not even your country."

The defiant, liquid look in his eyes showed how badly he felt about my response. "Remember 'Be bloody, bold and resolute'?"

"Sure. Shakespeare."

"Of course. But for years I thought it was you talking. It was only after reading *Macbeth* that I realized you were quoting. You were always saying that—always after me to do my utmost."

"I didn't mean to sacrifice your life, for God's sake."

"I'll give you another quotation: 'Some act of bloody resistance is needed. The bottle is corked, and only force can uncork it. But the violence, in order to succeed, will have to be committed by *unknowns*— not recognized enemies of the regime.'"

"It's not me this time."

"No, but it's from a book you gave me. I read it all the way across France—finished it in Rome."

"Michaelis's memoirs."

"Remember the part about sitting in the Colonels' prison? When he was deciding what he'd do if he ever got out?"

"Except Michaelis isn't a Macbeth," I said, grasping at straws, "he's a Malcolm, a peace-bringer."

"You think so? Who do you think informed the ESA

about Yannis' arrival at the airport?"

"Surely not."

Nick shrugged. "I don't know. That's what people are saying."

"That's crazy. Why would Michaelis do such a thing?"

"The people in Vouliagmeni think he wanted a martyr for the Left. And he could screw Panagoulis in the process."

I was silenced. Nick went on:

"But I'll say this about him—his book opened my eyes to something. The dictatorship had lasted so long, the Greeks had resigned themselves to it. They'd never get rid of the Colonels by themselves. It had to be done by 'unknowns', just as Michaelis said. An outsider."

"And you cared that much?"

"I'd listened to you and Mum talk about Greece for *years*. How much it meant to you, how you wanted to come back some day, even live here. I never heard the two of you be so passionate about anything. Ever."

But that was *our* life, I wanted to say, *our* passion, *our* folly, not yours. As for Michaelis, he certainly didn't mean you should become the next Hellenist martyr, the next Byron....

But I didn't say any of these things. The truth was, Nick had always been the best proof of Una's and my passion—for Greece, as for each other.

And for all I knew, Michaelis had had someone exactly like Nick in mind when he'd written his call to arms. Or when he'd betrayed poor Yannis.

I heard myself saying, "Una will be awfully happy to see you again."

He shifted uneasily in his chair. "How is she, anyway?"

"Worried about you. But apart from that, fine. I think."

"Do you still see her?"

"Not often."

He shook his head. "I don't get you two. I don't see how you could stop caring for each other."

"We haven't. We just can't stay married any more."

"It's so weird. You know, there were actually times when I got sick of her telling me what a great man you were."

203

"She said that?"

"All the time. When I was young." He paused, looking into the lantern flame. "Anyway, I hope you and she aren't expecting me to go home right away. Because I'm not." A matter-of-fact stubbornness had entered his voice.

"Why?"

He turned his face to me slowly. "Same reason I didn't want to leave Athens."

"What's that?"

"I want to see more of Maria."

*   *   *

He glared at me, waiting for me to say something, to challenge him. I didn't. Suddenly, volition had drained out of me.

So he just sat there in dumb defiance, refusing to explain himself, until I felt overwhelmed with frustration and despair at the absurd inarticulateness of fathers and sons, grown men who still haven't learned how to talk to one another — our usually glib tongues mute, mutilated, like Friday on the desert island.

Finally, Nick couldn't stand the silence either: "So why shouldn't I see her?"

"I didn't say you shouldn't. But you should know something, Nick. Maria was my lover once."

"What's that got to do with me?"

"She was the reason I left your mother."

"So?"

"So she's hardly someone you'd want to be close to."

He shrugged. "Really? I don't see why not. I like Maria — a lot. She's a fascinating person."

"How can you forgive her?"

"*Forgive* her?" He lurched out of his chair, started pacing around the kitchen. Finally he wheeled on me: "God, you're an asshole!"

His mouth began to work, as if he were trying to swallow something too large for him. "Jesus," he said then. "Jesus,

I'm sorry, I didn't...."

He was eyeing the doorway, flight on his mind. I stood to block his way but he was too quick for me, brushing past, rushing right out of the kitchen, out of the house, into the night.

*   *   *

I sat there irresolutely. Finally I followed him outside. While darkness had been falling, a wind had come up and was now driving the sea against the rocks, a pattern of muffled explosions succeeding each other a few seconds apart.

I hurried along the dark path into the village. I went as far as the old woman's grocery, its door closed, candles visible through the window, before I felt sure Nick hadn't gone that way. He must have taken the road in the opposite direction.

Then I remembered there was no opposite direction. I cursed myself for not keeping him in the house — not insisting he stay to finish talking it out.

Returning, I searched around the outside of the house. Was that Nick crouched against the wall? It turned out to be an old rain barrel. I remembered the stretch of beach along the water and rushed there, but in the moonless dark it was impossible to see anything. Going back inside, I retrieved the kerosene lantern from the kitchen. I was beginning to panic. What if he was more unstrung than I realized? What if he did himself some harm?

Of course. The rocks in front of the house. Above the water.

Setting the lantern on a ledge of rock beyond the front door, I hoisted myself up the side of the first massive boulder, then eased across an incline on the other side. I considered going back for the lantern but decided against it; it was too heavy and awkward to carry, I'd be too likely to lose my balance and smash it. So I continued over the rocks, unable to see very far ahead, holding my arms out at my sides, palms down, for balance, feeling with my feet for a flat purchase.

Eventually I reached the farthest of the four pillars supporting the balcony. The incoming tide shuddered against the rock wall a few feet below me, hurling spray that soaked my feet and pant legs. I had my bearings now. The blackness had begun to seem normal. And at last I saw the pale glimmer of Nick's shirt.

He was sitting on a flat ledge of rock above the water, looking out at the phosphorus-fringed waves rolling in, a semi-circle all around the cove. His knees were drawn up under his chin.

I clambered onto the ledge and sat down beside him. Although I couldn't see his face, I could sense his feelings with uncanny clarity right then. I visualized him shrinking away from me in repugnance. But I had to engage him. It was either that or lose him.

"So you knew about Maria all along," I ventured, yelling a little above the sound of the waves. "Who told you?"

"Let's forget it."

"Was it Maria? Did she talk about it?"

"She never mentioned it."

"Who then?"

"All right. It was Mum."

So Una had blabbed my little secret. How long ago? How long had I been desperately covering up something that Nick already knew?

"So…didn't it make you angry?"

Grudgingly, he turned a little, peering over his shoulder at me. "Angry at Maria? Why should it?"

"Well—she broke up our family."

"I always thought you and Mum did that."

"If Maria hadn't come along, maybe Una and I would still be together."

"I wouldn't know."

I didn't either. But there was something more I needed to find out, and so I pressed him: "Nick, what is it about Maria? What do you want from her?"

"I already told you: I just like her. She's unusual. She was kind to me. Isn't that enough?"

206

"Have you ever—" I hesitated, then plunged on, abandoning the safe ground: "Did you and she ever make love?"

The question seemed to startle him, then shock him into uncontrolled movement. "What are you saying?" He scrambled to his feet. "What do you want!" he yelled down at me. "What are you trying to do to me?"

I stood and faced him. "I'm sorry," I said, "that was really uncalled for. I guess I'm upset. I thought I was losing you again. Let's forget I said that, okay? Let's just go home. Come on back to the house and we'll make some plans."

Slowly Nick backed away from me—one step, two, three, until he was far enough for safety. Then he called in a low, even, strangely deep voice, "I'm not going back with you. I won't just…give up and quit. Like you did."

He turned on his heel and strode away furiously.

When I saw him do that, something snapped in me. I went after him. Catching up to him, I grabbed his wrist as he was raising a leg to hoist himself up another rock face. I wanted to force him to stay, to hear me out.

He just tore his arm free. He reached up the rock and with swift movements climbed to a higher ledge, but so precipitously he couldn't see where he was going. In the process, he lost his footing. Pirouetting above me like a dancer on the lip of rock, he regained his balance, then somehow lost it again. The soles of his shoes must have been wet, the rocks slimy with seaweed, because his feet went right out from under him.

He flung one arm outward in an attempt to break his fall. I lunged in the same direction, extending an arm to stop him, as he began slipping down the seaward face of the rock. He clamped one hand onto my wrist to break his descent, his grip so tight he almost pulled me down with him, but some blind instinct for self-preservation made me keep my footing, toes curling into rock. Losing his grip on my wrist, he plunged down, skidding over the steep seaward rocks feet-first. His feet hit something but didn't hold. Then he was gone.

I looked over the edge as far as I could. It was so dark down there, I couldn't see. Or it was the jutting angle of the rock blocking my vision. I had to go down after him.

Moving more quickly than I would have thought possible, I made myself descend the wet rock face, sliding from niche to niche, finally dropping the last couple of feet to a shelf of rock right beside the water. The dim, hollowed-out space was immense. Crouching, I couldn't see Nick. He didn't call out, didn't make a sound: there was no sign of him, only the sea thrashing. He could have a concussion, I thought, feeling blindly over the rocks with my fingers and toes, could be lying unconscious in the water, at this moment could be slowly drowning, pulled away from shore by the waves, and a low animal moan erupted from somewhere inside of me.

Down on all fours, I called his name. I looked desperately into the black water right in front of me. A cold wave leaped into my lap, spread over my chest.

A voice emerged out of the darkness behind me: "Why didn't you tell me about her?"—the voice changed now, plaintive, charged with pain—"Why didn't you? I needed to *know*."

I turned around and said to the darkness, "I see that. I do! For God's sake, Nick, forgive." The wind snatched my words, hurled them back in my face, shoved them down my aching throat.

Laboriously he pulled himself up onto his haunches, into a crouch. He held this position for a moment, testing the strength in his legs, ensuring nothing was broken. Then he sprang at me. I had no chance to brace for his attack—to prepare to defend myself against him before he pushed me backwards into the churning sea—but as his body struck mine, I realized he was flinging his arms around me, holding me, burying his wet, stubbled, weeping face against my neck. He was protecting us both.

EPILOGUE

Nick and I stayed three days in Maria's house.

We spoke no further that first night, not out of anger—that was all spent—but out of sheer exhaustion. We discussed only which rooms we'd sleep in off the upstairs hall—not our plans for the next day, or week, or lifetime—and fell into bed.

In the morning we were both famished. We shopped for whatever we could buy at the old lady's grocery. Together we cooked a remarkably good meal out of our limited ingredients on the gas burner. We went hiking over the dry, thyme-scented hills, swam off the rocks in front of the house, ate some more, and talked, but in a very different vein from before. We began to know each other for the first time as two men.

I was coming to realize how healing anger and anguish can be when expressed to the person who needs to hear them. All my life I'd shunned such feelings, or at least their utterance, religiously. I hadn't known the terrible cost, hadn't understood how emotions I'd always considered unworthy are indispensable to a life that's lived, not merely endured.

By the third day it seemed time to let Nick go; and to go my own way as well. It was still important for him to return to Athens, to take leave properly of the friends he'd made there —not only the couple who'd sheltered him in Vouliagmeni, but Maria herself. I knew I had no say whatever in this, yet I no longer saw any harm. My problems with Maria, my past, weren't his.

In the shabby little terminal on the outskirts of Iraklion, we shook hands, then, sensing this didn't quite express what we meant to say, hugged each other quickly. Nick used the open ticket I'd brought to fly to Athens, continuing a week later to Toronto. I was able to book a flight home for the next day, via London.

Once back home, Nick moved in briefly with his mother while arranging his return to school. It seemed right that he stay with Una and not me; it meant she'd get all the details and nuances of the story directly from him, and I knew she'd trust his version far more readily than mine. Eventually, he decided not to return to university right away, writing instead an eloquent and persuasive letter of application to Frontier College, an organization that teaches illiterate adults, offering to volunteer for a year in the north, or on an Indian reserve, or wherever they needed someone. His offer was accepted.

I wondered how much he'd tell his mother about the part Maria had played in his adventure. Finally I found out. Una and I had begun a *rapprochement* of sorts after I decided to stop going cold turkey on women; she accepted an invitation to lunch one Sunday at my apartment—a big change of heart for her, since she'd always regarded my place, however mistakenly, as some sort of passion pit. I was changing my attitude, too—feeling it was all right after all to live alone, to accept that apartment of mine as home, not purgatory, and invite people into it from time to time.

Over lunch, I related my version of the story in detail. It cost me something: the journey had been a painful one in many ways, but I tried to omit nothing. This was unusual in itself. I'd always assumed Una wouldn't countenance my discussing Maria in front of her.

Still, she wasn't quite prepared to let go of the old bitterness. When I told her how astonished I'd been to discover Nick already knew about Maria and me, she instantly reddened, in that grimly familiar way that had once upset me so much.

"Of course I told him. Did you expect *me* to keep your little secret? After you left us, Nick was terribly disturbed, desperate to understand what was going on. But you weren't levelling with him about Maria and you. You just acted all wounded, as if you were the one in pain."

"You think I wasn't?"

"I know. But at the time I had to tell him. Otherwise he'd

think I'd broken up our family by driving you away — Bad Mother. I couldn't have him believing that, now could I? I couldn't let you get away with that one too."

"Indeed," I said.

We talked a little more on the subject. Una made reference to Maria's evil ways, her doubtlessly suspect intentions towards Nick — understandable enough in the circumstances, I supposed — and I tried to explain that it wasn't like that: Maria wasn't the terrible person she imagined.

But after a few attempts, I could see there wasn't much point. As we all do, Una preferred her own version of reality, however black and white it might appear to me. And that was fine. In the end, it no longer seemed to matter that she and I saw things differently. There was still a lot I liked about her. I valued the chance to share experiences with her sometimes — a novel sort of pleasure. Although she'd once been the world to me, I could now enjoy her as another human being, a visitor in my world. It was enough.